Advance praise for *Living on the Borderlines*

"The stories in *Living on the Borderlines* cross bloodlines, heart lines, and cultural lines, powerfully charting what it is to be human in a world that works to divide us."
—**SUSAN POWER, author of *Sacred Wilderness***

"*Living on the Borderlines* is a hauntingly beautiful collection of stories of contemporary women and girls who live in the spaces between the reservations and traditional Indigenous territories and rural and urban communities stretching across western New York to the Blue Ridge Mountains, and beyond, to the island of Haida Gwaii off the coast of British Columbia. Despite the family choices, personal losses, intergenerational and historical traumas that separate Melissa Michal's characters across time and space, both they and their stories are woven together by their ancestral bloodlines, spirits and voices that dance and dream, spelunk and sing them from the past, through the present, and into a resurgent future. Michal's debut is a stunning achievement."
—**NIKKI DRAGONE, visiting assistant professor of Native American studies, Dickinson College**

Living on the Borderlines

STORIES

MELISSA MICHAL

FEMINIST
PRESS
AT THE CITY UNIVERSITY
OF NEW YORK
NEW YORK CITY

Published in 2019 by the Feminist Press
at the City University of New York
The Graduate Center
365 Fifth Avenue, Suite 5406
New York, NY 10016
feministpress.org

First Feminist Press edition 2019

 This book was made possible thanks to a grant from New York State Council on the Arts with the support of Governor Andrew M. Cuomo and the New York State Legislature.

This book is supported in part by an award from the National Endowment for the Arts.

First printing February 2019

"Phillip" was first published in the summer of 2010 in the *Florida Review*.

Cover art: *Dawn Song* by Natasha Smoke Santiago
Cover and text design by Suki Boynton

Library of Congress Cataloging-in-Publication Data
Names: Michal, Melissa, author.
Title: Living on the borderlines / by Melissa Michal.
Description: New York, New York : Feminist Press, 2019.
Identifiers: LCCN 2018017739 (print) | LCCN 2018020406 (ebook) | ISBN 9781936932474 (E-book) | ISBN 9781936932467 (trade pbk.)
Subjects: LCSH: Six Nations--Fiction.
Classification: LCC PS3613.I344437 (ebook) | LCC PS3613.I344437 A6 2019 (print) | DDC 813/.6--dc23
LC record available at https://lccn.loc.gov/2018017739

To my mom, who never ceases to believe in me.

*To the many mentors, good friends, and guides who
encouraged me along the way and who spoke kind words.
You will never know how much those words have meant to me.
Each of you is in each line, each word, and each intention.*

And to my namesake, I have missed you always.

Contents

Living on the Borderlines   3

The Long Goodbye   6

A Song Returning   27

The Carver and the Chilkat Weaver   47

Calling the Ancestors   79

Nothing but Gray   82

Towpath Lines   109

Crowding the Dark Spaces   118

The Crack in the Bridge   140

Luck Stone   153

Phillip   169

Morning Smile   195

Dancing Girl   210

Acknowledgments   213

Living on the Borderlines

Living on the Borderlines

Standing at the water's edge, the line remains invisible. He can see the line, a mind map. But he also knows why the line exists and who placed it across his nation. That would explain his heightened awareness, but it does not explain why he sees this line everywhere, over most images his eyes bend and send to his brain. This space. He visits other places and does not see lines, not even state or other nations' lines. Just their own land. Right there.

Mohawk. His inherent ID. His community self. He considers this each day when he wakes up. Of course, many daily things disturb these thoughts. Work. Money. Food. Cars breaking down. His child crying. His wife touching his shoulder, her hand shaking.

The shake is temporary, based in fears that sometimes cross her mind. She worries the food will not always be enough.

He does not allow empty plates. There is always food. But they skate that line.

The St. Lawrence River flows over the borders. Now Canada, now US. The line is somewhere down the middle, where canoes once traveled back and forth, routes from one Mohawk village to another. From their nation to other tribal nations beyond, with borders mutually agreed upon. So long ago.

Nighttime and dawn are quietest. When the sun has disappeared or just risen, the world there changes and withdraws into itself, renewing, connecting, and recreating. The river glows then, and so do the lights of houses and the few motor boats that pass during those times. Red lights and white and sometimes yellow lights skimming along black water.

He paces along the river. Change is inevitable. His mother taught him that. Change comes whether you want it or not; it's simply how you deal with those evolutions. He isn't looking for the canoes to return to the water, like they presume.

He wants the lines gone. That simple. Disappear from his vision.

One whole nation again among six nations.

Blinking, he imagines that.

Blinking again, the lines come back.

Reality of divisions and lines forced on him, on them, literally and legally. *Their* laws.

His wife comes up behind him, encircling him with her arms.

Where'd you come from? he asks.

I knew you would be here. She pauses. Tightens her grip for a moment and then stands beside him. The river is beautiful now, she says.

He stares at her face. The lines go away. They don't exist within or around her. Or their children.

What are the kids up to?

With mom. She's putting them to bed. Thought I would join you.

He comes there so often. The bridge looming over. Maybe not that spot. Maybe further down. Or another area. Or a drive away. The river calms him, gives him pause to think and to remember.

She hasn't sought him out before. She leaves him to his moments. But he likes this. Standing there with her now, her hand on his back.

He pulls her closer and shuts his eyes. Her warmth spreads across his side.

What do you see out here? she asks.

Water. Wind. Boats. People rushing about. Or stopping to see the people around them or with them. Lines. Borders. The hard stuff comes to me, then leaves.

She nods. We can cross when we want.

True. But it's not so easy.

The lines are not ours.

No, but we should do something.

He blinks one last time. His vision clears. Let's go home, he says.

They hold hands, meandering back. He enjoys her voice rising along the edges, crossing the water.

He knows the lines will be back.

He squeezes her hand and she leans in.

The Long Goodbye

Today was a quiet day. Nala stood by her grandmother's door. Morning shadows pulsed along the walls and mottled her grandmother's forehead as she sat in a rocking chair by the window. Nala didn't understand why her grandmother spoke in streams one day and the next day, silence held her. She couldn't be comfortable in the stillness when the older woman watched out windows for hours without moving. She was sure she made less noise padding down the stairs, so careful.

"Your grandmother was forever changed when she left her family at twelve," her mother had said when Nala was thirteen, the first time she noticed her grandmother's moods.

Nala saw then the exhaustion in her mother's emotionless eyes and the dark circles underneath.

"Nala, we have to respect how she is and how her life evolved." Her mother flicked soap suds off her hands and picked up a dish towel, rubbing it up and down her arms, then put her hands on her hips.

"But you didn't know her back then," Nala said.

"I know her now. And I may not have been born yet, but I knew her then, too, in how we are connected."

"But that was so long ago. Why is she still like that?" Nala asked.

"Sometimes things stay with us long past the time they should," her mother said. "And we can't let them go."

That was how their conversations often went. Words, then silence.

She felt her daughter stare after her. Longer than normal. The screen door shut behind her as she carried laundry to hang on the lines. In the summer, their dresses and pants and shirts swayed in the breezes that filtered through the tall pines and oaks. This space was hers, and the *clip-clip* when the clothes went up satisfied her. She wondered if Nala would see the world around her. Maybe she had sheltered her too much. Nala floated in that in-between: a young adult, not teenager, but not really adult either. She had married by her daughter's age and took care of her mother during rough times. There was no lazing about then. She and her husband agreed not to let Nala grow up quite as fast. Though, she had never questioned her own mother, whose spells of quiet had affected their connection too much and switched their roles.

Nala disliked how their underwear became white flags for all to see. Their neighbors didn't hang laundry; they used the dryer like everybody else.

"The wind is free," her mother said.

"Really, Mom," she would retort. "Wind."

Nala remembered during her childhood her grandmother letting the breezes wash over her face and body. So happy.

That morning, her parents had spoken quietly in the kitchen about her grandmother. Their words carried into the dining room, where shadows covered Nala.

"Things are getting worse," her mother had said.

Her dad's tone seemed light. "She always comes back." Nala could tell he tried to hide his emotions.

Her mother and father grew up on the Cattaraugus Rez, where everything sounded like make-do to Nala. She'd never been there. They moved before she was born, although they didn't get far. Bloomfield, New York, was only a few hours from Cattaraugus. Her grandmother and grandfather came as well, filling each space in the small house with only two bedrooms and an upstairs den, which became Nala's room. The added sliding pocket door, which made it appear like a room, often echoed in Nala's dreams. Her mother had picked the house for the trees surrounding the yard and rounded hills rising beyond. She once said they were the people of the hills.

A year ago, days before her grandparents' wedding anniversary, her grandfather passed on. Her grandfather, too, had always been quiet, although naturally so. Somehow, her grandmother's spells had never bothered him. He knew about them when they married. Nala never could figure out how he remained so patient. No complaints. He touched her grandmother on the shoulders and the arms, stroked her hair, read her poetry by Nora Marks Dauenhauer. During spells, he had to coax her out to the car. He would talk softly and get her to come downstairs or leave the house much easier. Her grandmother's spells had become longer and more frequent since her grandfather's death, and now, Nala wondered if she would stay in her quiet. It seemed like her grandmother recognized the dates this week. She seemed more retreated in a way Nala couldn't explain—but felt. Maybe that was why she passed by her grandmother's room and didn't walk inside. What was really left of the woman who used to laugh so loudly?

Before he died, her grandfather told Nala that she must care for her grandmother more. He had noticed how Nala tiptoed around her quiet times. He could pick up on people and their feelings. When she was a little girl, Nala loved the connection. He soothed her woes before she even knew to cry or be sad, stroking her forehead with the swirls of his fingertip. His actions had annoyed her as a teenager because she didn't understand how he knew her troubled thoughts, how she wanted distance from her family. She didn't want the college experience or a degree stamping approval on her life. His eyes would move from quiet to disappointed any time she avoided family or tried to decide her future. Finally, as she entered her twenties, she learned to block her thoughts from him and put her walls up.

He felt the block. His eyebrows would rise and then fall, hurt.

"We all have our ways of connecting with this earth," he said.

Nala still hadn't found hers.

Her grandmother stayed quiet throughout the week. But today, she walked downstairs after some cajoling from her mother and stood by the kitchen sink, staring into the flowering lilac trees. Her grandmother's fingers pressed against the brush she circled on the dishes. Nala thought this might mean her grandmother would come back that day or the next, and she waited for those days. The heady scent of the lilac trees swirled around the room.

Nala left her and her mother in the kitchen and drove her grandfather's car down to the lake.

The second-growth pines lining Canandaigua Lake pointed up to the sky. Blue water pushed through the branches at breaks in the tree line and sparked with sunlight. There were no easy view points along the road.

After twenty minutes, she pulled over, her tires crumbling gravel and grass.

She had been ten the first time she stopped at this spot on the lake.

Nala watched from inside the house waiting for her grandmother to come in and maybe play or cook. Most days then were good. Her grandmother would pull herself up onto the large riding lawn mower, her hair tidied back under a handkerchief knotted at the nape of her neck. The silky polyester kept the curls she had spent time rolling in metal rollers from waving away in the wind. Even on the plastic yellow seat, she could sit, shoulders back. Hours later she would come back in the house, giving off a sharp country scent, a mixture of sweat and grass.

This time though, her grandmother insisted they get out of the house.

"Let's go for a drive."

Nala trudged over to the car, her grandmother convincing her to leave. She pulled the seat belt over her shoulder and clicked the metal. Her grandmother smiled, the curlers gone and a green scarf covering her waves.

"Roll your window all the way down," her grandmother said. She turned the handle, cranking the window down into its secret compartment.

Nala did the same. She had been intrigued by the disappearing glass since quite small. She poked her fingers down in the crevice. The rubber liner on either side felt funny, like it could steal her finger if she left it there too long. But the space where it divided drew her to play with it each time and to wonder how the glass safely moved up and out of its hold in the door.

"Here we go!" Her grandmother hit and pumped the accelerator, lurching the car and sending them both reeling forward.

Her grandmother could drive!

Nala's eyes became large and darkened brown. The ride went like that as they curved around the lake. Somehow her grandmother knew how to take the road at just the right speed so Nala felt the ride in her belly but wasn't knocked around. The woman behind the wheel was not her grandmother. This woman's face lit up with life. Her smile curved large enough to create dimples, and her cheeks turned pink and pretty. The large sunglasses she wore made her look like old Hollywood. She laughed a laugh that emanated from deep within.

"Whew ha!" her grandmother exclaimed. She turned to Nala and poked her. "This is it, isn't it."

Nala smiled and nodded while still holding on to the door.

The overlook only showed the south side of the lake. You couldn't see the whole lake from any one spot on the road. You would have to go higher in the hills, she supposed. Nala sat on the car's hood. The old metal held up under her, not giving in like some of those newer cars built for better gas mileage. The trees stood quiet. Not one catch of a breeze stirred through them or over the water. A raven cawed in the branches, and somewhere a blue jay purred and cried on the other side of the overlook. One lone chipmunk squeaked in high-pitched intervals, chattering warnings.

Eventually the animals quieted with the stillness of the air. She could feel the connections her grandmother had talked about during those rides. It wasn't about nature healing her—how Western. The stillness and the trees focused her thoughts. Her grandmother was good at reading the energies around places. And her grandfather was good at what was inside of people. A balance.

"You Indian?" a boy had asked Nala in high school. He stood next to her locker. Assumptions about her heritage happened more often than she liked. Her skin was a bit more olive toned, but not as much as her mother's. Kids, and sometimes adults, often told her it was her eyes. The almond shape and her long lashes. She shook her head. They knew she went to powwows after a teacher had asked her about them once.

His elbow leaned high above her head against her locker.

"Yeah," Nala said. She turned to walk away. Her long black hair floated around her face.

Snickers from his friends followed her down the hall.

"Hey, Indian, take me on a nature *vision quest* or to your powwow." He began to dance around the lockers, chanting.

Seriously?

Her mom experienced similar stuff in high school. Each time she came home with a story about some Native joke, her mom would stroke her hair.

"You're better than that. Just ignore them." Then she kissed her on the forehead and patted her arm.

Sometimes Nala envied her family members who looked

whiter and who didn't go to powwows or act "Indian." She would sigh and trudge back to her room.

She wanted wiser words—some cure-all for the world's stupidity and ignorance.

Her grandmother patted the hood of the car. They were looking out over Canandaigua Lake that first time, Nala's fingers still playing with the window.

"Sit here, Nala." Her grandmother leaned back on the hood, splaying her hands behind her. She lifted her head toward the sky and closed her eyes. Wind blew her hair from under her scarf. Her grandmother untied the silk and let her short hair fall away on its own, laying the scarf on her neck.

"Does Grandpa know you drive?" Nala asked.

"You know," said her grandmother, "I come here and drive around the lake because I can feel things here. Past times. That sort of thing."

Nala peered at her grandmother and couldn't make out if she was serious or joking. *Feel things?* She raised an eyebrow. Her family didn't outright talk about ancestors or all that stuff. It was like somehow she should just know it automatically; that made Nala uncomfortable.

"Mom, why can't you just tell me who we are exactly? What our community means?" Nala had asked a few weeks before her grandmother's drive. Her arms flew out along her sides and then fell. She shook her head.

Her mother stared at the floor a moment, then sighed. "I have always told you things."

"You code it."

With the side of her hand, her mother brushed breakfast crumbs off the table.

"I listen, but you never say anything." Nala let out a groan. "What are we, stoic Indians?"

"You need to go out and experience it. You know, go to the dance group or with your grandfather on his walks."

Nala rolled her eyes. "I do that already. Is that the only way to *be* Indian?"

"No." Her mother's voice turned soft.

"You don't go."

"I'm here with your grandmother." Her mother watched the back of Nala disappear. She wanted to explain when Nala was ready. The trouble was that she had learned by just being. She hadn't had a discussion either. There was no easy lecture on being Seneca. And there was no easy way to *be* Seneca.

Her grandmother seemed to be reading her mind because she looked at Nala for a while before moving her eyes back to the lake. "If you sit here and listen, you can hear the vibration from each being," she said. She never said more than that and rarely moved. It took a few weeks of returning to the lake, sometimes to different spots. But Nala began to understand.

The first thing she felt was the trees. The feeling did not exist in voices—not like a human kind of speech. The presence wasn't the trees, though. She recognized they were related to her, the things behind the feelings, and, as her grandmother had said, the vibration. Then she could also feel it from the breezes on the lake and the birds. That vibration flowed through her and stirred what she could only explain as her blood. Maybe it wasn't her blood stirring with the vibration, maybe it caused the vibration.

A few more summers moved like that. In the last days at the lake, the brown in her grandmother's eyes became lighter and she raised her right eyebrow in approval. Nala held a knowing that teenage years and fears would later erase.

The last time at the lake during that period, the two had snuck back into the house. Her grandfather was still in his chair, reading the paper right where they had left him when they snuck out. Nala caught him winking at her and nodding approval.

When she returned from the lake that afternoon, laughter drew Nala into the kitchen. It told Nala her grandmother was returning, for now. Her mother and grandmother worked at the stove and counters, chopping peppers and shucking corn. Her grandmother deftly cut off the kernels.

"They have cans for that," Nala said.

She kept cutting the ears and smiled. "Not as fresh or sun warmed."

Nala set the table, one, two, three round plates, all different colors. Her dad had left that weekend for some big powwow in Arizona. The ingredients swept off the boards and simmered in pots, becoming salsa and chili for dinner and appetizers the following week.

"Your dad will miss my chili," said her grandmother.

"He asked you to go with him," said Nala.

Her grandmother shrugged. "I'd rather be here." She motioned for Nala. "I'll teach you how to make fry bread."

She had her mix the ingredients until they became crumbled bits and then, finally, a soft dough. She worked at it with too much force until her grandmother steadied and slowed her movement. She put her hands over Nala's.

"You have to want the dough to work with you." Her grandmother's hands were warm, and they pushed the dough over and over, a steady movement.

Nala didn't really want to make this bread. Not with its history. She was the reason why they never made it together before because she avoided it.

"Add flour," said her grandmother. She added even more to the counter after Nala put some down.

As instructed, Nala rolled the dough until it became a large ball. It felt smooth and chill to the touch.

Her grandmother broke off a few pieces from the ball. She kneaded one into a smaller ball, sprinkled some flour on it, then flattened it into a small, thick disc and poked a finger sized indent in the middle.

Nala got handed another ball, an indication to follow her grandmother's lead. She worked the dough in her hand. Her disc ended up looking ill shaped and uneven. But it still entered the pile ready for frying.

The pan fizzled as each piece of dough cooked. Browning discs sent rising bread smells into her nostrils, turning her stomach with hunger pangs.

Nala worked the dough until there was no more and her fingers felt numb. Much of the pile, though, came from her grandmother's speedier work. The bracelets on her grandmother's wrists jingled and shone silver in the fading skylight. The frying continued to surround Nala with sound. As breezes wove through their yard, sounds came into the kitchen, almost like crying as the screens and curtains moved.

Nala paused a moment as the sound of frying entered her ears and pierced her eardrums. She held a disc of fry bread over the pan, but couldn't drop the final piece in. "Why do we make this?"

Her grandmother raised an eyebrow.

"It only carries pain, you know," said Nala. She couldn't hold this in any longer, her anger at the silence, at things she spent hours googling on her own, rather than hearing family stories.

Her grandmother stopped kneading, then started again after a long silence.

Nala's mother pulled her into their living room—the dough dropping to the counter. "Do not speak like that to your grandmother."

"It's true. Why can't we speak?" Nala rolled her eyes. "She won't break."

"It brings back things she must forget to be okay."

"This is stupid. We sell that stuff to white people at festivals, powwows. They eat our past. We didn't have that flour or lard before them or before the long trails." The people getting government rations along the trail or on reservations took the offered flour because there was nothing else. Their food had all been stolen, or sometimes even burned by raiding military. She tried not to think about her community eating unnaturally, but it pushed through.

"I know. She knows. Leave it there." Her mother dropped her arm and walked back into the kitchen. Her grip left finger marks still imprinted on Nala. Her mother stopped and turned back. "You know, they buy. Yes. But we sell fry bread to push away the sorrow, not take it back in. They'll swallow that, and then maybe know what we know."

With shades pulled down to keep the room cool, the dark of the living room gave way to an empty air Nala felt drop. Her shoulders down, she turned her back and went up the stairs. Her mother's shoulders gradually sagged as well, and she walked back to her own mother. But she listened for her daughter's steps, hearing sadness in the slow footfalls.

At dinner, Nala sat down late. Meat and spice crawled up to her room as a reminder. The two women already eating stopped conversation when she put her napkin in her lap.

Her grandmother nodded at her. "I was just telling your mother how she snuck out to see your father. We had to put bars on windows after several times."

Her mother flushed, and her grandmother laughed.

"Fighting was part of her growing."

Nala and her mother exchanged looks. The chili seemed like something between soup and stew—filled with onions, peppers, tomatoes, ground bear, corn, and beans, but thin in the sauce. The liquid trickled down her throat, burning in the way she liked, filled with her grandmother's choices.

Chatter began again, with Nala silent and listening. Her mother and grandmother laughed as they easily returned to the past with their words. She could tell her mother missed these talks with her own mother as she leaned closer to her grandmother. Nala and her mother barely had an affectionate relationship.

"Nala," her mother said, "why don't you check in on Maria Jimerson this week? I've got a package for her anyway."

Nala sighed. *She's weird.* All Maria did was talk. She could be there for hours listening to stories she knew nothing about.

"Hey," said her mother, looking sharply at Nala. "She needs people. Besides, you need to keep busy."

Her mother referred to her many jobs she quit that year.

"Mom . . ."

"You were always so good at science."

Nala's stomach tightened. Science had come easy, but the answers never gave her a knowing that made her want to be a doctor or nurse. "Okay. But just dropping off the package."

Her mother shrugged. Then she and her grandmother turned to laughter again at an old high school tryst her mom had had with a boy before her dad.

That night they all turned in later than usual. Her grandmother had seemed especially happy and had been the one who kept them up. So, when screams awoke Nala, they shocked her. The sounds weren't human. She rushed to where they emanated from: her grandmother's room. Her mother was already there, trying to hold her grandmother down.

Her grandmother went from quiet to damned—clawing the air to fight or to breathe. She was out of her bed and by the door. Her eyes were black and charged with such hate. She howled and screamed, trying to get out of the room. Nala backed away.

Her mother's eyes seemed to say, *Help your grandmother.*

Nala ran out of the room and back to hers. Her mother's voice carried under the doorway, calm and kind until her grandmother stopped the abrasive sounds and cried.

She heard her own heartbeat through her ears. It took a while for her breathing to slow. The quilt filled with purple hills her grandmother had made for her mother when she was young comforted Nala just enough to fall asleep. But not before her mother sang soft lullabies in the other room in a tongue foreign to Nala, but familiar.

The following morning, her mother handed her the package for Maria Jimerson—an indication Nala wasn't to wait all week.

"How's Grandma?" Nala asked.

Her mother picked up Nala's cereal bowl and glass and dumped them into dishwater. She shook her head. "Go to

Maria's," she said. "Go." She waved her hand, shooing her out of the house like she used to do when Nala was little and underfoot.

She couldn't look at her daughter.

The package for Maria was square, wrapped in brown paper, and fairly lightweight. It didn't seem to contain anything that jostled around. When Nala stepped up to her door, it opened almost immediately as if she had been expected. She had always thought Maria strange. Her mother had known this woman since she was a child. Maria, though, moved off the rez first. According to her mother, Maria had never changed in either attitude or appearance. Her long hair was gray and darker gray, her eyes black in a way which didn't seem to come from happiness.

Her mother once told her, "Maria went to the schools, too, just like your grandmother."

Nala had asked what the schools were like, but her mother stayed silent each time. Eventually, Nala stopped asking.

Maria motioned for her to come in. Nala held the package out to her, but Maria didn't take it. Instead, she motioned again for her to come in.

Tea enough for two people sat on the table. "Sit," said Maria. It didn't seem like no was acceptable.

The package sat between the two of them.

"How's your grandmother?" she asked.

Nala shrugged. "Okay, I guess."

"She still having those nightmares?"

Nala was surprised; Maria took the silence as yes.

"Early days were tough," said Maria.

"I wouldn't know." She looked out the window to Maria's backyard. She had a clothesline; a small sparrow perched on it for a split second. He flew down to the grass, where other sparrows plucked at tiny blades.

"In certain ways, you do know, I think."

"I *don't* know what you mean." Nala sipped her tea, scalding her tongue. She blew on it several times.

"Your grandmother's ways are a direct result of what they did to us," said Maria.

Nala tried to block this woman who seemed to be reading her thoughts. But she could feel Maria's force. She was stronger than her grandfather had been.

"No one was allowed to interact with family or friends. We lost our tongue to speak our language. All this, you must know."

Nala nodded.

"Our history doesn't mean anything without the stories."

Nala felt Maria again, this time her eyes, not her thoughts, penetrated.

"The first thing they did to me was cut my hair. I saw these pointed objects coming at me, and then felt cold run down my back. I still hear those snips. Metal and razors. My hair swung around my ears, and my arms became full of goose bumps. They ushered me into another room where I had to strip to my underthings. A woman inspected those and decided it was not enough, pulling the rest off me. Her eyes threatened even though I had no idea what she was saying. Their clothes were scratchy and smelled funny.

"I cried for my family and called out. The woman slapped me. Hard. An older girl put her finger to her mouth to quiet me. I learned later we couldn't speak our language. And I got slapped more times for speaking out. We slept in large rooms with many other girls who weren't our family. I knew no one. And my first months there, no other girl spoke my language. I was alone. That's why they had to kidnap some of the kids, like they did with your grandma, and take them far away."

A chill moved along Nala's arms.

"We are strong with family. We are not without."

Nala bowed her head and pulled at a hangnail. She had never asked her grandmother about those stories. *Kidnapped?*

"It's what happens inside a person that is hard to explain. What would you do if you were gone, if who you were disappeared? But yet your body was still here on earth?" Maria paused. "Nala, you have it easy in some ways. And in some ways, you have it harder."

"Harder?"

"You may have harder times accessing the old ways." Maria stopped to drink her tea. "She may have been beaten or raped, your grandmother."

Nala's heart hit hard against her chest. No one had spoken those words around her—and so matter-of-factly. "Did you go to the same school?"

"No, honey. She was older than me. And she got taken so far away. We don't know how she snuck back later. That's spunk right there. But those schools all had the same goal: to change us. Make us like them."

"So, are we like them now?"

"No. Some try, but . . ." Maria handed Nala a cookie.

The sugar sprinkled on top tasted sweet in her mouth, and the cookie crunched between her teeth. But the inside was soft, not too sweet. They sat in silence until they finished their tea.

Maria stood and cleared the table. "Come back again," she said.

Nala wondered what was in the package but knew she should go. She sat in the car awhile. When she returned home, she continued to think while cleaning dishes and wiping down the table. She couldn't get visions of the school out of her head. Visions of the students so young.

Her mother came into the kitchen from their yard. She must have been walking in the fields along the back. Nala had noticed she was gone and figured she was somewhere nearby. Her cheeks were rosy and pretty, while a small line of sweat beaded around her face. Nala's mother never went too far from the house if no one else was home with her grandmother.

Her mother stared at her. Nala glared back. She wanted her mother to know her anger.

"What's going on?" her mother asked.

"You knew. You knew all that terrible stuff about Grandma." Nala clanged dishes into the dish rack.

"What are you talking about? I told you about the schools. You knew what they did."

"I didn't know what they did to *her*." She faced her mother, hands on her hips. She read her mother's emotions in the way her eyes fell and her mouth quivered. "Why aren't you angry? Why don't you shout it around here so people know?"

"It's our family." Her mother moved toward Nala and touched her cheek. Nala turned away. "Those things don't need to be spread to the whole town."

"That's like lying, not telling me everything."

"I've never lied to you." The tone in her mother's voice chilled Nala. She moved toward the door.

"Mom, please don't walk away!" Nala shouted.

"She never told me what happened there." Her mother's voice barely whispered out the words.

Nala's hands slid off her hips.

"I can't tell you what I don't know. And just so we're clear,

23

your grandfather tried to talk to you. By the time you were old enough, you stopped being open."

"He didn't tell you?"

"I didn't want all of the details. He knew that." She turned the doorknob. "I get a pretty good idea from her bad nights. That's enough for me." Her mother left and headed toward the woods again.

Nala returned to scrubbing the dishes and could almost feel her grandmother doing the same. The circles she made synced up with her grandmother's patterns. Sorrow overcame Nala in waves. She hunched over and sobbed, tears mixing with soap. She kept scrubbing, though. Then she took out the laundry to hang on the lines.

A small breeze rustled through the trees and lifted the hair around her face. The clothespins attaching to the clothes and then the line made a consistent *clip-clip* that intensified as Nala quickened her pace. She stopped at the end of the first line and leaned on the post. What she heard in the leaves and branches sounded much like her time along the lake, except softer. She hadn't noticed that here before.

Nala pictured family she'd never known, how her grandmother's disappearance changed them, too, could even see her great-grandmother searching for years and not coming back to being herself again, either. She saw white people come and take her grandmother from the rez roadway. She saw her grandmother refuse their lies about her parents, kicking the man who held her. She saw dust piled up in clouds behind the car as it drove away, her grandmother's mother running after her until her breath gave out. And then she saw the dust behind her grandfather's car, her grandmother at the wheel.

Nala breathed and took in the vibrations.

Maybe the breezes would carry away this sadness. She knew the energies came from the bedroom upstairs, and maybe from her own letting go and giving in to the power of her grandmother's silence.

Wheels on the cart squealed as Nala pushed the TV stand into her grandmother's room. Her grandmother's eyes never left the window. The only things to move were the tassels on her purple shawl, which caught the breeze.

Nala slowly touched the tip of her grandmother's shoulder with a finger, then her hand, then the other hand, putting just enough pressure to knead the skin a bit. With a gentle pull, she lifted her grandmother out of the chair and guided her to another one in front of the TV. Nala sat on the bed, her hands splayed for support across a blanket stitched with the Hiawatha Belt. The video started automatically. She tossed the case on the side table.

Her grandfather had recorded odd shows and movies, almost like a special mixed tape that only Nala and her grandmother knew the secrets to. She fast-forwarded to the second listing: Charlie Hill's old stand-up. Her grandfather's scrawled blue handwriting was made tiny on the label to fit each title. The Oneida-Mohawk-Cree comedian had come to their town when she was just a toddler. Opening images and jokes across the screen did nothing to stir her grandmother. They ran over his tongue loose and easy. "We had a little real estate problem." She heard what he said. It felt like things she had heard before. She didn't remember his visit but had seen snippets when searching YouTube for other things.

Then, her grandmother laughed. She laughed and laughed and laughed.

Arms across her chest, her mother shadowed the door, and Nala nodded at her. Her mother sat down next to her grandmother and put her arm around Nala's shoulders.

Her mother leaned closer to Nala. She looked at the video case. "That's true." She tapped the young man's shirt.

The old video case, a mistaken swap from another she assumed, stopped her. Pulled her.

It was worn, almost falling apart. Faded in so many places. She knew it was a still from some cult American Indian movie. A skinny Native young man stood with loose, long hair in a bright-blue tee shirt next to two other people.

She picked the case up again and ran her fingers over the one image.

"Fry Bread Power," her grandmother said, seeing the phrase on the tee shirt. She laughed again and turned to her daughter. "Fry Bread Power." The smile remained.

When the comedian finished, Nala laughed. His last jokes suddenly hit. "Fry Bread Power," she said. She nodded at her grandmother. A taking it back.

Her grandmother's shawl moved again in the breeze. And Nala laughed again, full and deep. Her mother joined her, her eyes lit with brown flecks.

A Song Returning

She stood next to the bed. A green-and-yellow quilt covered the white sheets. The design was the plainest one she had seen her mother make. Mia didn't know how or where her mother picked up the craft. But suddenly one year when she was twelve, there they were on their beds for each birthday. The only present. Her two brothers just cast the quilts aside, Jeremy's blue and Nathan's baby blue. Delilah, who preferred Dee, got a red one. Even though she kept hers, Mia understood her expression. One of disappointment and sadness. The two had shared the same bed, one that pulled out from the wall in the living room. Her dad made the bed before he stopped visiting them. Dee kicked her almost every night. Now Mia's husband did the same.

What her sister's eyes said, Mia knew deeply. Her quilt had been the colors of midnight and silvery gray with intricate stars and hills. The hills stood deep in the apparent night, steady over everything. That quilt had made her feel safe, still did. But her husband preferred softer blankets. The quilt lay across the trunk at the end of the bed, a place where she stubbed her pinky toe often.

She grasped her mother's quilt, leaving the bed dressed in white. Someone else would be renting the space. Under strict orders from her mother, they were not to sell the land.

That space was their right and heritage, she would tell them.

Mia wouldn't ever stay on the reservation again. She couldn't raise a family in tiny HUD housing. She and Charley didn't have children yet. There were plans, of course. But the Creator seemed to have other ideas.

"Mia?" Her brother Jeremy stood in the doorway. "We've got to go. I think we found everything personal."

"This whole place is personal, Jere."

"I know," he said. He put his hand on her elbow for a hug. She stood her ground and he let go.

"She was happy here." She pushed her cropped hair behind her ear. The strands would get away again soon enough.

He picked up a medium-sized box marked Bedroom Clothes, Hair, and Trinkets.

"How?" But her words echoed to no one. He had already left. The trailer felt empty. Not simply lacking people. But energy. *Her* energy had gone. Even her perfume no longer hung in the air—vanilla, berries, sandalwood, caramel, jasmine. Her mother had this fire, a small one, but determined. She laughed so loudly. Every time she laughed, she could barely contain her body. It was contagious; people near her, too, would laugh for no reason. She even stirred food with vigor, rubbed Vicks VapoRub with the same force. Mia couldn't have helped but cough and cringe, her chest red.

A tear left her eyes. She wiped it away and took a deep breath, willing the tears to stop, to not come at all.

Mia latched the door and didn't look back. The sun falling

behind the trees brightened everything with yellow, just before the globe fell away into the horizon. Summer was leaving, but ever so slowly that year. The trees were still quite green and the air humid.

"We can come back, even with renters, you know. Walk the land like she used to." He shifted the car into drive. "She checked on things that way."

"I'm probably not coming back."

Jeremy watched his sister. He switched from the road to his sister. She sat, her back slightly hunched. Shadows played there. Mia had looked out for all of them, the next oldest under Nathan. He curved the truck, bumping over holes or rocks. The shocks bit right through him. He'd have to get that fixed.

No matter how happy her life was, his mom had been too young to go. She should see her grandkids born and watch her kids be happy. He never figured her for dying. There was no reason, they had said. Simply age. He ran his hand through his hair. Maybe her life had been too crazy with all of them in that tiny space wearing her down. That does something to you.

His eyes blurred with tears, which he of course held back. Driving kept his focus and the road merged with the darkness.

Once back in Bloomfield, Jeremy put the boxes in the guest room. Mia had already gone up to bed, saying nothing—the quieter one. Probably the closest to their mom, she rarely spoke up about herself. Mia and their mom had fought hard when she was a teenager, but after college, the two spoke every day on the phone. Mia visited when their mom couldn't get out her way any longer, later leaving her work as a nurse. He loved his sister for these things, her true traits. Then she brought her mom to this room. The bed and dresser in order, waiting for their mom's return. He thought he smelled her perfume. *Mom?*

He locked the back door and slid into his truck. When he

looked in the rearview mirror, a bedroom light was on and a shadow by the curtain. Mia was the one who watched for them when they got home late nights when their mom had early work mornings. Mia never did doze off in school after those nights.

He shook his head and drove back to his own family.

Mia couldn't sleep in bed with him right now. Charley didn't try to force her, and he never would. He fidgeted with his belt loops. He wanted his wife with him, just to comfort her. But sometimes she needed space. This was no exception. He watched her wander the house, as if looking for something she couldn't find. But nothing was lost.

The next morning, he scrambled enough eggs for a family, adding water to her approved fluff, hoping she'd eat two bites. Maybe even three. But she pushed them away and sipped on orange juice. Her silence and empty stare out the window nearly made him want to drop in the chair next to her. Instead, he rubbed the shoulders of a flimsy doll. Nothing to knead, not even a tension spot. Her body was just a vessel, empty of her spirit.

I can't.

"I'm going to grab some groceries, need anything?" The keys hung loosely in his hand, and he moved them between his fingers. The noise where metal hit metal sounded unpleasant.

No answer. Her back molded into the kitchen chair, filling its white lath spindles.

Charley paused. He waited for his wife to turn, just to see some light enter her eyes. She didn't. As much as leaving hurt, he shut the door.

When the door clicked closed, a more careful version of his usual slam, Mia stayed in that chair for another half hour. She knew he was gone. She heard him ask her questions and talk, but she had no desire to interact with the world. The quiet was comforting somehow. When the sun rose higher, brightening the trees, she put the dishes in the sink. Her slippers shuffled and swished. She left the windows shut, so the double panes kept out sound.

The stairs shifted and creaked as she headed upstairs. She sat on their bed. Her body had somehow weakened over the past seven days. The difficulty moving limbs surprised her. Her desire to remain asleep, to not want to get up, did not. She didn't like the control she lacked. But she let whatever this was—grief, sadness, anger—take over.

Wearing a white tee shirt, no bra, and cotton shorts, she trudged back downstairs, planting herself by the TV. At such an angle, she didn't quite get a straight-on picture. But the position meant she didn't have windows in her sightline.

Charley still hadn't returned after almost two hours. She checked her cell phone, but nothing.

A dish fell from the dishrack, clanging loudly along the steel sink. She hated that sink for many reasons. One being that noise. The other how easily the metal scratched and how horribly it stained. Mia sighed.

Her mother's perfume suddenly filled the air. The scent made her jump. *I'm going crazy. Crazy.*

Something made a loud thump.

For the love of Pete. This house. She changed the channel. But the show was some Lifetime daddy-murderer theme. Nope. Flip and flip again, until some house renovation show.

Another thump.

Is there some bird in the house, or animal? It didn't occur to her that the sound might be a human being until she got half-way down the hall. She took a kickboxing stance and threw a punch. Then opened the office door. Nothing. Only one other room was down there. Her mother's.

She flung open the door. The doorknob hit the wall and bounced back halfway.

Still nothing.

Mia searched the bed, dressing table, dresser, under the bed. She felt a large hardcover book, so she shimmied it out from under the bed's crevices. Rumi's poetry. Her mother had different tastes and knew classic literature. Where she found the time to know them, Mia couldn't figure out. Even when they were young, her mother was always reading some Jane Austen or Eudora Welty or N. Scott Momaday book.

She opened to the table of contents, running her finger down the page. Her mother had checkmarked her favorite poems. Double-checked one. Mia turned there.

An envelope was stuck among the folds.

A mild yellow or maybe cream, the envelope felt soft, but not delicate. She had seen her mother write on this paper before. She pulled out the unlined pages.

Darling Ella,

I think of you today. Your birthday came and went last week. I thought of you then, too. But I think I miss you more on the normal days. The leaves are changing. And the girls have all gone off to college. Everything is a bit emptier now. When Jeremy goes, I'm not sure what I will do each day. He's such a good young man. The other day, he convinced his sister Dee she should stay in college, do the things she does. She sometimes doesn't believe she can with her fears of failing. He has a gentle force and he brought out her passion. It's there, deep inside all my children. I would think, you too.

Always,

Mama

Tears streamed down Mia's face. Loud sobs escaped. They never talked about Ella. Silence was an accepted family reaction that came automatically. You just don't talk about the hard stuff. You leave it alone. She learned from aunties who said that very thing when she had hard days at school or a fight with her mother or siblings. If you let the hardships alone, they stayed far in the distance.

Her face wet, she flipped through each drawer. Opening and closing them quickly. Empty. Charley had cleaned out the drawers a few days before. He would have told her about any letters.

One of the boxes tipped over. That one held clothes. With the last box, and everything else strewn across the bed, Mia held her breath. But there they were. Tied with rubber bands, or string, and some with large binder clips. *How often did she write?*

Charley found Mia, envelopes piled around her, unopened. She sat with her hands behind her, stabilizing her body, and probably her mind. Her eyes weren't empty any longer. But they weren't full either.

"Mia," he said.

She shook her head.

"What is all that?" He kept his voice calm. This worked the rare moments she got distant. Things had to be big for her to pull behind this curtain.

He took the envelope she handed him. The original one.

"Oh wow. Mia?" He sat down, his hip touching hers. "She never showed them to you?"

She mouthed no.

She had once told him about Gabriella. He somewhat understood the situation. But he couldn't understand giving up a child. No matter the money or space. But her mother had arranged all of it, quickly too. That was all he knew, and all Mia knew, he presumed.

"Did you read them?"

Nothing.

He rubbed her back and left. He soon came back with a sandwich. She fingered the bread and pulled out the Swiss cheese. Her favorite. He made sure there was extra, with a touch of mustard. She didn't come up to bed. He thought he heard thumping below around three a.m. But he fell back asleep.

The next morning, he stood in the kitchen, scratched his head and his arm, then grabbed eggs. He didn't see her at the table. Papers spread out, lined up in some order, with their envelopes touching the pages. She held a cup of tea and had a light bathrobe around her.

"She wrote sometimes once a week, sometimes once a month." Her voice was scratchy, her eyes darkened underneath. "She couldn't send them, I guess. We never knew where Gabriella ended up with just a first name."

He picked up one letter, Mia's sixteenth birthday. Another, a planting at Ganondagan. Then dancing. The paper seemed milky smooth. Her handwriting was sometimes easy and flowing. Large loops. And others, closed and small, hard to make out.

"You need to tell them."

"Not now."

"Did you read them all?"

"You know, she used to pull the covers up to Dee's and my chins. Tuck us in and tell us we were special girls. Each time she said this, I could fall asleep easily. Just a simple phrase."

"This matters to them, too."

"I don't know what she said to the boys. They were in the back."

"She loved each of you. Even Gabriella."

"Maybe her more."

Dee's mouth gaped open. The letters on the table made her want to touch them. But Mia's organization kept her from that. They were so delicate looking.

"What do they say?" She couldn't take her eyes off the table. "Where's Nathan?"

"Coming later," Mia said. "He knows. I told him."

Jeremy had read some before Dee came. She couldn't believe he was so calm. This was huge. Big. She didn't remember Ella's birth. She was tiny then. And really, until now, she barely remembered being told she had a sister. *How do I feel?* she asked herself. *Weird.* Someone out there was related to her other than their one true aunt. But she might never know her. She wasn't sure it mattered that she meet Gabriella. *What would she even be like?*

"Mom made sure she went somewhere special," said Mia.

"What does that mean?"

"They swore she'd be raised Seneca. Taking her to events, dancing, volunteering. All those bits. Going to the cultural centers."

"We might have seen her, then? And how is that being Seneca?"

"I don't know, Dee. Maybe."

Mia's tone told her that they hadn't seen her. Maybe she had been somewhere, but they were five minutes apart, coming and going. Or maybe by days or weeks.

Dee dropped a letter back on the table. She barely read the page. Enough to know that her mother cared for Gabriella. "I miss you today, Ella." How much of that took away from the four of them present, right there with their mother? "It's always the youngest."

"Dee, come on," said Jeremy.

He might have been the youngest before Gabriella, but he scolded more than her mother ever had. Kept her in line. She shivered and wanted distance between them. That happened sometimes. "Close," their mother often said. "True family sometimes gets too close. A little irritation shows we're on the right path."

She missed her mother so much her body ached. But Mia, the family rock, had checked out. Jeremy's tone and the way he touched Mia told Dee he tried to take on the role. Mia just kept quiet and held everything in, so ready to explode.

Jeremy worried some about Dee, yeah. But more so about Mia. Dee could fall apart with one touch. But Mia so rarely retreated. *And where is Nathan?*

Some pans rattled and Charley quickly threw together hamburgers, corn on the cob, and frozen French fries. Jeremy liked this guy. He took care of things without asking. Read people.

"Meal of champions," Jeremy said. He bit into the corn and ate one cob standing while Charley set up a toppings station. The kitchen counter was cluttered with silverware, dirty dishes, and ketchup, mustard, tomato slices, pickles, lettuce, cheese, and chopped onion. He stood taller than Jeremy, who generally felt short around anyone, but Charley had a wrestler's body and height.

Charley leaned against the counter, arms crossed. "Think you guys should look for her?"

The girls were in their mom's room, checking for more letters.

Jeremy shrugged. "She hasn't been around. Would she even accept us?"

"Does that matter? Isn't it about making a connection now?"

"She'll be nothing like us." He crunched a pickle between his teeth, the sweet juice waking up his taste buds and even his brain.

"But she *is* you. Even with a different raising."

"I don't know. We just lost our mom." *We could lose this sister, too. All over again.*

"But gain a sister." Charley slapped Jeremy on the back.

Jeremy thought he felt cooler air wash over his body. Shivers shook his back.

"You all right, man?"

"Yeah. Yeah. Let's put some burgers together." The cold air wasn't unpleasant, just sudden. Jeremy's blood felt warmer, like a heater turned on somewhere. Maybe he'd read more letters after dinner.

Rain began pouring, tapping on the windows and roof. The sudden temperature difference frosted the windows with steam marks. That unexpected summer chill. They ate in silence. Anyone watching who knew them would think they had gone strange. None of them could find any words, which made Jeremy twitch, all of them cramped together at the kitchen table, rather than the formal dining room.

Nathan showed up as Dee and Jeremy were almost headed out.

"They're just letters, guys." He tossed a letter down. "She was always bad at letting go of stuff."

"Sisters aren't just stuff," Jeremy said.

"Do what you want." Nathan ate a leftover hamburger, slathered in mustard and cheese and slapped between two thin bread slices. He caught mustard and wiped his chin with his finger. "It won't change anything. She still died."

"Mom would have loved us all together again." Mia put her hands on her hips. She sighed. "Maybe we owe this to her."

"To who, Ma or Gabriella?" Jeremy said.

"Ma. But Ella too."

Nathan shook his head. "No. We don't owe people. We lived there. Now mom left there. It's best."

Mia yanked the hamburger out of his hand and threw it away. "You're mean. That's all. Always have been."

"We grew up in shitty places. Now we live a little better. So what if it's mean to say those things."

Jeremy held up his hands. "Let's come back to this another day."

"No," said Nathan. "Let's just get beyond this. That's that." He made a cut-off motion with both hands.

Charley and Jeremy exchanged frustrated looks. Nathan

could tell Charley held back his words. But he didn't care. He almost wanted the guy to tell him something so he could give it right back. His muscles tensed and the veins in his upper arm showed. He met Charley eye to eye. Mia's husband had nearly punched Nathan several times. At their wedding, he had pulled Nathan up by the lapels and shook him.

"You should go," said Mia. "It's time for everyone to go."

"Yeah, yeah," Nathan said. He left, the door slamming.

Now Jeremy wanted to smack him.

"That went well," said Dee. She hugged Mia. "See you later."

Charley and Mia heard both car doors thud shut outside.

He made her chai tea, the kind that smelled like Christmas, and set it down. She pushed the mug away.

"Maybe he's right. Maybe she wouldn't even want anything to do with us."

"She'll know it's important. That would seem unlike your family, otherwise." The last comment he filled with sarcasm. *That Nathan.*

Odd, but Mia wanted to sleep in her mother's room. Under the green-and-yellow quilt.

"Come up when you're ready."

Charley often fell asleep early, whether in a chair watching TV or putting on his pajamas. *Farmer's hours.*

He approached her in the Fairport Library. They had both been wandering the DVD section. She remembered running her fingers across each case, trying not to miss a single title. He had walked past the rows so fast, she wasn't sure how he even saw the titles. He had stood out, though, probably because she caught sight of his bright blue eyes. So clear. And those smile lines around his mouth.

"Are you going to get that one?" he asked.

She had tilted *Alien* but wasn't sure she was in the right mood. The cinematography and plot were dark, more serious than she needed that night.

"I guess not." She handed the case to him.

"Charley." He held out his hand and she shook it.

Slightly rough, but soft. A tingle ran through her arm. The skin, the blood. He blushed.

"Nice to meet you," she said. She could feel her cheeks get hot as well.

"Here, try this one."

Roxanne. "Never seen it."

He gave her his card, and she got one last touch. Another tingle. "Let me know if you like it. I would love to hear what you think."

That night she twirled the card through her fingers as she watched a man help another man vie for the woman he loved. With a long, unusual nose, he didn't think the girl could like him. She laughed so hard.

Their first date was a movie, *Independence Day*. He even slept through the end, while she remained riveted. She secretly loved action movies. Turned out, he didn't.

Mia knew she was safe so long as she was with Charley. His large arms enveloped her. He insisted on paying for everything. With his own large Puerto Rican family, he seemed to understand hers much more than any other man had. The emotions, the heated arguments, the closeness.

Farmer Charley. Yet he was an engineer. All those numbers must tire him.

She trudged up the stairs, still pulled toward the back bedroom. She wasn't sure, but she thought she heard singing. Mia touched Charley, just a light one. He turned and wrapped an arm around her shoulders. She sighed and fell asleep.

Charley awoke and heard Mia crying. A gentle sound he might have missed if he hadn't been out of REM. The sun streamed through an open curtain he must not have drawn completely. He never minded morning sun. The warmth kept him from sleeping too long. She'd roll back over, though.

"Hey," he whispered. He touched her stomach and pulled her against him. She quieted, but still shook. Silent sobs. Brushing her hair back, he kissed her cheek and waited. Just held her. Soft breathing told him she had fallen back asleep. Usually he would get up and make breakfast, start the coffee. But he remained awhile. This wasn't a deep or content sleep. Her brows furrowed and she twitched in moments.

He finally rose, dressed, and made coffee. She thrived on schedules. Although, she sometimes craved spontaneity, which she really only used to surprise others. Right before her mother passed, he had planned a trip to Alaska for them, July, the warmest month there. It was supposed to be a surprise. The travel company understood and put everything on hold. Waiting.

He knew her whole life had been on hold. Taking care of brothers and sisters. Making sure they went to college before she did. Taking care of her mother. Putting off having her own children. There was so much between them she didn't say about her childhood. He made every attempt instead to read her, intuit body language.

When they would go walking Saturday mornings and the green leaves appeared brighter, readying for fall changes, her eyes drifted off. She had told him she felt closest to her ancestors then. Harvest time. She would curl up in the quilt her mother made her once back inside those days, even before she passed. He could tell she needed that closeness. His touch didn't affect her when she went somewhere in her head.

They talked about everything else.

When he asked Jeremy once about their childhood, her brother shook his head. "It wasn't bad. It just wasn't good. She had that all on her shoulders, man. All of it."

"And your mom?"

"Working. Cooking. Taking care of the neighborhood."

At some point during her childhood, Mia simply stopped talking about herself and only made mention of others.

Charley had tried. Oh man, how he tried. Trips. Gifts. Nights out. She would check her phone, though, or refuse the money spent.

Sneakers. Water. He was ready and headed out. Charley looked up to their bedroom window. No movement. He couldn't fix this. Charley nearly broke when his grandfather passed near his twenty-third birthday. Most from that period was fuzzy. This might be different. But he got it.

The darkest woods enveloped him as his body disappeared, taking his usual route.

Mia rolled over and touched the empty pillow, still warm. Charley's cologne clung to the sheets, fresh like clean soap. Arms stretched, she pulled her body into a straight line and rotated her feet and legs.

The full coffee pot brought a smile. This morning, she poured it black. Medium roast with a slight nutty flavor nearly burned her throat. But she didn't care.

She couldn't read the letters again. They told her that her mother never let Ella go, never forgot. But that didn't surprise her, even if she hadn't known. Her mother always had cookies for the neighbors, fed the kids she knew probably hadn't eaten that day, and sometimes gave their toys to the family a half mile down the road. Her strength emanated through her actions. People felt comfortable in their home and often stopped by or spoke to their mother in the street. Tight didn't mean without. But she also remembered the years her pants no longer touched her ankles. That happened many times. Her growth spurts came earlier than Dee. Once they stopped in high school, Mia had no more problems. She wore more skirts and dresses. That ended the nickname High-Water she had throughout middle school.

Another sister, though, and Mia knew it wouldn't have been possible. One more mouth, more milk, more hot dogs, more rice. More clothes and toys. She understood better than Nathan was willing.

A voice sang. Low and sweet. Maybe Charley had left the radio on. Or maybe the neighbor's music filtered through their closed windows. She lifted the living room window. Just birds, small sparrows, flitting around.

The back room again.

Maybe she wanted so badly for her mother to be there, she imagined the song and the voice. Could she have also conjured up her perfume? The scent clung to the air as if her mother had just sprayed the bottle. Not some far-off, left-behind smell.

The song rang familiar. Mia couldn't place a name with the tune or recall the words. She wasn't even sure there were words. But her brain told her, *Yes, I should know this.* Just as quickly, everything—song, scent—faded.

Nathan had been there the day Ella was born. He was twelve, she ten. Their dad had already left. Nathan whispered to her one night while brushing teeth that he knew their dad was gone for good. "All these kids," Nathan said. "Too much noise. Too much crying. Not enough space." He spit into the sink. But his words sounded like spit, too. Harsh and full of bite.

Their mom cried out in the middle of the night. It was too late to drive her anywhere. "Boil water, Mia. Grab fresh towels. Sanitize the scissors." Labor didn't even keep their mom from a level head. She walked Nathan through everything, holding Mia's hand, until Ella slid into his shaking arms.

He wrapped his small sister in their best towel, the fluffy green one. Ella cooed. She barely cried, just stared at her brother.

The doctor later came and left, saying they didn't need the hospital. "Good health," he said. "Surprising." He glanced around their trailer.

Mia frowned. The trailer may have been crowded, but the space was impeccably clean.

Nathan rocked Ella. She quieted when he held her.

Months later, their mother announced that Ella would need to leave. "Go live with a good family. Have a good raising."

"But we do just fine," Nathan said.

"Of course we do, Nathan." Their mother put her hand on his shoulder. He shrugged her off and slammed the screen door behind him. He never held Ella again.

Two months later, a family picked her up, promising a Seneca raising, with their values, songs, dances, everything they could even though they weren't Native.

Their mother still sang them to sleep, words they didn't recognize, but stopped when, at fourteen, Mia told her to go away. She literally pushed her off their bed.

"Mia, how could you tell her that?"

"Go to sleep, Dee. We just need to sleep."

She couldn't remember what made her do that. Maybe

hormones. Maybe being worn out from schoolwork and housework. Later she missed the songs but couldn't bring herself to ask for them. When her mother thought she was alone, Mia heard her sing with the radio, swinging her hips a little.

The tune from earlier that day came back. There seemed no source but her own mind. She knew though she didn't imagine the music. Mia lay down, her body on top of the quilt, her side arching perfectly into the already-formed mattress dip.

"Do you remember the night Ella was born?"

Dee coughed into her tea. "Mia? What is this?" She switched her cell phone to her other ear.

"Nathan. He basically helped birth her."

"Wait, what?"

"Yeah, he did. Cut her cord. Wrapped her up."

"That actually explains a lot. More than his reaction."

"I know."

Dee thought she heard the old Mia returning. A strength in her sentences she couldn't explain. That made Dee feel safer. Did in high school, too. She could count on her sister and knew she could figure her way through any of Dee's problems. Dee certainly didn't lack them. "Do you think this will make him worse?"

"I don't think anything will make him better. Especially now Mom's gone."

"Dad maybe?" Dee checked a text that came in and itched to answer the message.

"No. He went looking for him, I don't know, maybe six years ago. Untraceable."

"Wow. How did I not know?" Dee threw her phone a look. *They never loop me in.*

"He made me swear, Dee." Mia's tone shook.

Dee sighed softly. "Okay. What do we do here?"

"Do you want to know her?"

"Sure." Dee shook her head no, though. *I'm a terrible sister.* Maybe she could. But what difference would meeting this other sister make now? Gabriella didn't know the rez. Or what they went through.

Mia touched the letters again. The paper felt smooth, pleasant to touch. Her mother's window overlooked the entire backyard, the woods, and the hills. Probably the best view besides the back bathroom. The house had a strange footprint, with sitting rooms and a kitchen in the front.

She set out her mother's hairbrush, a mirror, and her pad of paper and pen.

By talking to her siblings, watching their body language, and having read them their whole lives so they avoided trouble, Mia didn't think they cared to meet Ella. Maybe Jeremy. Something kept leading her back to the letters, though.

"Charley? Hey, Charley!"

"Hey, hon," Charley said, drying his hands with a dish towel.

"I think we should call that investigator friend of yours."

"Really? Okay. I'll do it now." He smiled.

She nodded. He noted a small light turn her brown eyes caramel.

Her mother's perfume returned. *I've got this, Mom.*

The Carver and the Chilkat Weaver

Calluses bumped in rough familiarity with each other. The couple, side by side, hand in hand, walked down the cleaning-supply aisle. Fingertips barely touched palms with hands that fit. The grocery store, although filled with fewer than six or seven other shoppers, appeared crowded. Someone else in every aisle they moved through.

Their cart rolled, overflowing with more food than they could eat, while Aaron pushed fingertips to the handle bars. Lettuce, tomatoes, salmon, pasta, chips, pops, rolls, sandwich meat. All for the party next week.

"They still laugh at us. And stare," Anna said. A wary up-then-down glance passed from a new neighbor.

"You know, they're not laughing, hon. It's you. It's that hair." Aaron winked at her.

Her smile spread slow. But the full stare now illuminated in her pupil revealed she still knew better. Her skin lay pale and bright next to his toffee hue.

When they first married, the smallness of the store had made her feel large, as if she stood out every time. She found it family-like, with cashiers and associates knowing everyone by name and food preference. Maybe that was why it grew to annoy her over time, like only family can. Small town. Small Haida Gwaii.

Aaron stared at his wife's profile as she bent over the deli counter and peered through the plastic. She stood a bit taller than him, even in flats. Her red hair shone as brilliant as the morning she had first strode into his shop, though a few grays strayed through her thick mane now. Curls that popped up in the rain framed her face. He heard her repeat her dread of the wet that caused this, rain that poured consistently in their region. He could look at her all day, standing back and waiting. A smile spread when she learned her favorite cheese remained in stock that week. Jonathan at the counter remembered to order it; she didn't have to ask. The island offered these small moments and pieces of joy. Flights and boats brought things over from the mainland across Hecate Strait, and you took what came in this way.

He saw that she seized moments a lot like this—took whatever happened and simply strode on through it. And the strength that carried he admired as much as her green eyes. Those eyes knew him well. She paid attention. And she remembered even what he didn't say. The closeness that was so frightening in the beginning now comforted him.

They weren't the kind of couple who finished each other's sentences. But thoughts they read by a simple gesture or look. A familiarity from years of listening when there were more words.

Leaning over the wallboard, digging into the carving lines he made, he scooped out wood with his bent knife, clearing layers of years, still never quite reaching the oldest section. But it was down there. He knew that.

When he drew sketches, he imagined a clean piece of wood, not necessarily free of imperfections, but a starting place. Black pencil scrawled across white drawing papers. These were the official work drafts. Sometimes he found scratch paper and doodled. Scraps of these fluttered out of various books over the years. Square recipe cards, oblong envelopes, magazine ad tear outs—all with his pencil marks. Much of it remaining on paper—not moving to wood grains.

The pieces he carved were most times commissioned by businesses and organizations, some non-Native, some Native. None of the pieces were completely and utterly his. They would hang or stand where he might never see them. He ran ideas by whoever paid him. And tweaks came from them, not the elders or the clan or the family—but those commissioning. The work brought in money. That was what colonialism added to their culture—basic living needs. He sighed. Maybe there was no way back to the way things used to be. Shaping the wood was honor bound, still a privilege to carve something.

He tired easily. It came from his knees and his fingers. That meant less patience—sometimes even for carving. He could ignore the signs of growing old with warmer weather. But the fall moving into winter sharpened his aches. Seasons came much sooner than they had in the past, at least in his mind.

He leaned into the current wallboard—a cruise-ship commission. June heat invaded the workshop, a large comfortable building with high ceilings. Light poured through the line of windows facing red cedars, shore pines, and triangular mountain crevices. He enjoyed this quiet. But the shed was owned by his employer. Really the only way he could have a shop like this. The penciled designs marked carve lines. As he chipped away at a fresh spot, it seemed like the adz didn't move—merely nicked the wood. But the consistent motion in one place slowly gave way to depth. This made him push harder, to see the adz move into the tree's veins. His elbows, shoulders, and hands took over.

The wallboard lay horizontal, parallel to the floor on slats and joints that held its pieces waist-high. Each section contained its own support. Put together, they would eventually be the length of a small fishing boat. Once he made his way to the middle of the piece, Aaron climbed onto the wallboard, pulling up and crawling to the center. With the adz again, he did the same thing, following the veins. The view seemed different to him, like he was in the piece himself. A 3-D man, kneeling, almost prostate to the board in a prayer to the Creator, his hand closer to the iron portion of the adz, his eyes steady on the design. Intent. An eyelid appeared here, a head there.

Pricks and needlelike pains collided up one muscle and then another. His legs and knees grew stiff. He did this in shifts, up on the board, then down next to it.

Last section. Last section.

"You could retire," Anna had said a few weeks ago. "We could get by. You've done this so long."

"I've got to keep it alive, you know. This way of showing our honor and our people."

"Alive for who? You've had many apprentices."

He turned to her and smiled. He recognized that she was not close to understanding this. He didn't mind. She came further than others. She was indeed part of their family, now

Haida, adopted into the eagle moiety, he raven. These two communities within Haida culture were like relatives. They took care of one another and married from within each other's communities. They had important responsibilities to each person, each family. She simply did not grow up with this notion. But he knew that if their ways were not done traditionally, people would think they had disappeared, vanished into the grain of the wood. Only to be speculated on by art historians and anthropologists who simply didn't know how to even try to understand. Anna tried, though.

"And there are new artists dispelling the myth of the *disappearing* Indian," she continued.

"Ya." He rather liked the pluck of the artists who were more contemporary. Their designs almost unrecognizable. But his lines, his carvings, moved so far back in the Haida way that he just didn't know how it all compared. Or what it meant to be keeping things as they were. The contemporary carvers' messages and their questioning were not his purpose. It was theirs. He built history in his mind—something from the past still proceeding into the future. A portfolio to be replicated in the carver's own eyes of course, but carried on.

She tried. Anna tried to live the life—thirty-five years later. And most days she succeeded in being a part of the small island and it being her home.

She arrived in Haida Gwaii in 1975. She had heard of a man carving totem poles, and that intrigued her. A practicing artisan—someone to engage with rather than study from a book.

Women did not carve, and she wanted to know why. Nor did they design the weavings or the design boards. Yet, they wove the baskets, the Chilkat robes, headdresses, leggings.

They did beading, ceramics, and quillwork. But the designs, the designs came from the men.

It was like her, then, to jump on a plane and seek the answers, rather than call or write a letter. This brought her to Aaron's workshop. She expected some older man, gray and bent over. His black hair, thirty-year-old body, and coy grin made for unexpected pleasure.

She told him her thoughts on the absence of female ideas in their art. He laughed deep in his belly and tilted his head. "You'll need to learn some things," he said.

They married in six weeks. He knew, he told her. "You don't wait when it's right. You go for it. And I had to find some way to keep you here, so you didn't go back."

"Aaron, I'm white." Well, really, she was, but wasn't. She was mixed. But her family didn't count *that* side. Once her grandfather had told her she was Seneca, descended from him, which in a matrilineal society meant that she lost her heritage, her card so to speak. That was all she knew. At the time she didn't see it as something she was disconnected from, merely something she wasn't a part of. Such a quiet man and caring. More of his money was spent on other people. Her parents hated that.

"You're Irish. American Irish. Yes, that is too bad, isn't it?" Aaron chuckled. "So. Love's love, eh." And that was that.

From the beginning, neither talked about their backgrounds any further. She just happened to be living within his and taking that on as part of herself. She felt less uncomfortable with that as time moved forward, years molded into her the island, the people, and the ways life unfolded there. She accepted these ways.

Because she didn't count her Seneca heritage, he didn't, either. He had raised his eyebrow when she told him. She waved her hand as if to wave away that side, just like her mother when Anna brought it up during her teenage years. She appreciated that he never said anything about her family or background. A quiet agreement to build their own family.

He always seemed sure of each move. If he sketched it out, Anna noticed, he acted on it. And she could tell when he sketched in his head. He rolled his eyes up to the sky, stared for a moment, and came back down with an idea. She observed those traits the first week.

She found security in that. He checked himself. He thought about ideas. About important things.

Anna didn't think before flying to Haida Gwaii, landing in Skidegate. And she didn't think before attending Boston University, or leaving it. She went. Off to another of what her parents called "silly escapades." They rarely visited her in Boston, and then never on the island. But she thought carefully about marrying Aaron. Not because marriage meant leaving college. But because she had never wanted to settle down. It would be a slower life. She could do that. In the back of her mind, maybe she wanted to stop all of the flying about, seeking answers to her many questions—that led her to want marriage and Aaron and no more scattered self.

As much as her parents detested Anna's escapades, they were the cause, always being off somewhere without her since she was ten. She remained behind wondering what the place was like, who they met, what they did there. Answers to the world. And that pulled her to India, Mexico, Venezuela, and Haida Gwaii.

She didn't need answers with Aaron. Although he patiently answered any questions. Those questions waned and then disappeared as the island gave her answers.

Anna thought of all those first moments as she steeped some tea. A touch of sugar, but mostly the broken mushroom pieces, dried, at the bottom adding flavor. All this in his usual red mug.

She found him on their deck, scribbling and then pausing to watch the eagles. Tonight, they caught unending currents above the trees. Their feathers glinted in the fading twilight, tipped by the dusk. A light that would never quite darken this time of year and would remain half-gray. His stare intensified on eagles and then paper as he deepened himself into the lines of the sketch. She set the mug next to him, and the smell of earth and decay rose from the steam, hitting her nostrils. He nodded and winked and put pen back to paper with his other hand on the mug handle. When he lifted it to his lips, he sighed.

She smiled. The wink turned her heart. So many years and it still did that.

Back in the kitchen, she scrubbed the dishes with soap. Warm water coursed over the bristles and ceramic. The window in front of her gave way to pines and yellow cedar and salmon berry bushes. Squirrels and birds and the occasional black-tailed deer picked at the berries, content perhaps to share the red-and-orange tartly sweet fruit. Their backyard, as small as it was, became her favorite spot over the years, how it changed in the seasons, but didn't. The same could be said about the people and the culture of Haida Gwaii. Perhaps that was why she succeeded at living some place so different from herself. To be who she truly was here, rather than be who she wasn't. Nobody minded that on the island.

She contemplated Aaron's design of the Chilkat blanket she

had woven her first years there. It hung in the room off of the kitchen, the room with the most light and space.

Light shone through the windows in Aaron's apartment. Even after a year of marriage, she still couldn't quite call it her own. The dappled shadows moved across her painting, darkening colors in some places. She dipped her brush in water, turning the then-red liquid purple.

She arched her back and stretched her hands behind her. It wasn't done. But everything she could do in that surge had emerged on the canvas. Anna left her stool and put the teapot on to boil.

It was a small studio, but the ocean rolled over craggy volcanic rocks scarcely beyond their entryway. When she looked out, it almost seemed like the apartment expanded. At some point, maybe they would have a house with a deck and more space. But she didn't think she could simply give up being steps from the water, where she could see black points stretched out to sea and feel the salt entering her lungs.

The spoon clanked against the mug to keep the ceramic from cracking under intense heat. Earl Grey wafted up to her nose as she unwrapped the tea bag. Waves lapped along the edges, and she could hear their slow, but constant movements. A raven's squawk followed. The clear, cold air never got old. Although she missed the deep warmth of the summers when bones finally thawed.

The painting remained in her mind. It changed as needed to become what her hands would stroke onto the canvas. Aaron had been trying to talk her into weaving as well. But she couldn't stop painting. It lived in her fingers and danced out through her brushes. Adrenaline pushed on and filled their walls. A mix of his carvings and her paintings.

The doctor's office shrunk that day—as if it had been some optical illusion before—now tiny with three people and little air. The same doctor who cared for his nieces and nephew. When they found out Anna could not conceive, Aaron read her posture as both relief and sadness.

He watched her eyes move in and out of darkness that day, staving off what she might be denying, he thought. She had often said before this moment that she couldn't become her mother. He knew she wasn't her mother, though. With his nieces, she was even more beautiful—purely giving. They were her own family, not simply *like* her own family.

They were in their late thirties. Much too late. There wasn't anything to be done—not with their budget. They considered adoption. But her mother had a stroke months later, and Anna stayed with her for a year. This changed them.

The time apart made Aaron restless, and he wondered if she would come back. Phone calls came few. And Anna's voice shook when she spoke. He could have traveled with her and taken a break from commissions. No was her consistent answer. "I have to do this myself." The stubborn fight he loved turned in the other direction.

Aaron kept working the year she left. He often caught himself stopping at the small bedroom built into their own. It had never been decorated. But intentions seemed obvious. She had even bubbled with excitement over colors.

Before her mother's stroke, he rambled on to Anna about who would take on his carving. Who would he teach in their family? His two brothers and sister, Donna, had daughters. His other sister did have a boy, John. But he refused to learn any Haida culture.

"I tried, Aaron," Anna said.

"I know." He wanted to take that back, that moment. He forgot himself, her grief, within his own. And then she left.

When her mother died at the end of that year, she returned to the island. She hadn't told anyone of the death or her return.

"It's not the same here" was all she said for weeks. He figured she meant without her mother.

Adoption left the table after her return. Anna's silence clearly desired a shift in life plans.

Most of the time, family gatherings occurred at his brothers' or sisters'. Something was going on every month or few months. His siblings' homes could hold more people and still breathe a little. But now and again, Anna would host in their tiny house anyway. People spilled into every nook of the two-bedroom space from living room to porch to kitchen and dining rooms.

Guests milled in front of the food and along the chairs and walls. A rumble followed the bodies of people—laughter, talking, whispers, children tagging other children—moving through the walls and creating waves of sound.

Anna always held the get-togethers in the warmer weather. Their deck and yard then acted like extensions of the house. Aaron built the deck shortly after she returned from caring for her mother. She could sit in the Adirondack chair, now a faded aqua, all summer barring a downpour. Their house sat high enough that, although the view was mostly green yard and woods, on tiptoe she could make out lapping water that melted into the horizon. During certain sunsets, she caught green flashes that lit up the water, dividing it from the far beyond.

The colors struck the valley and ocean every night with different fires. Sunsets never got old.

Seawater smells drifted in, although roads and fields away. Her body begged, though, to toe-dip mornings, just as she did at their studio. That same saltiness floated from the pots of clam soup and teriyaki salmon. Pasta salads mixed in color with the desserts and the cans of pop in ice buckets.

There were more cousins standing around the barbecue, cooking various meats, loud belly laughs crossing family barriers of arguments and time. It seemed those were left at the door of their parties. One man wore a Hawaiian shirt with bright-pink flowers. Anna covered her mouth to hide her laughter. Most wore jeans or khakis and tee shirts. This was not the group she grew up with, who so often dressed in the latest styles with heels, skirts, ties, and dress pants. These women instead wore tops and scarves with the formlines, finelines, and ovoids forming whales and bears and eagles. They were supporting local artists, fashion marking family rather than trend.

She told them, "Don't bring anything." They always did. They came bundled down with children and some type of food or paper product, making the tables multicolored and full of flavors.

It was at these times that Anna didn't mind the crowds, not like at festivals or the store, where things closed in on her and space mattered. In this house, space was a commodity. And elbows and backs met often. To her, this house felt like a cocoon. Yes, odd. But similar to the idea of swaddling babies. The tighter they were wrapped, the safer they felt.

She navigated through the kitchen, to the dining room, to the living room, to the porch, and then back to the deck off the kitchen, checking in on each person. Did they have drinks, food? Were they having fun?

"You fuss. Every time," said Aaron. He tried to push her into a chair to at least "rest for five minutes."

"I've got this, Aaron."

"They know you keep a good house." He gave her a look that meant concern. Where his eyebrow moved down, rather than up.

"We got too old for this," said Aaron.

"Never," she retorted with a slow smile.

A few times a year this event proved to pass time in a different way, with weeks of preparation, the actual party, and then the clean-up. Her body hummed in one place and didn't itch to ferry out to other places. They used to take small trips to Prince Rupert or Vancouver. And a few times to Sitka in the States. Not so much anymore.

"This salmon is truly delicious," said Donna. She shook her head and gave Anna a hug.

Donna made probably the best salmon on the island. Anna blushed.

Little ones crawled across the furniture. And Aaron's niece, Nari, her niece, too, she guessed, brought her daughter, Lily, over and put her in Anna's arms.

"Here," she said. "Enjoy baby time."

Donna raised her eyebrow. That physical admonition did get old fast. Anna could read her thoughts. Could she handle kids emotionally if she couldn't have her own? She had been "handling it" at every family gathering for years with no breakdown or tears. But they still worried. Not everyone in the family, really only the older siblings. Youth seemed used to bouncing back these days and didn't see her that way. And it wasn't that she didn't want to adopt. But by the time she had decided for sure, she felt old, too old for someone new to teach everything to and chase around. The need to mother left her. Just like that. One day when she was forty-two or forty-three, she felt it lift out of her soul and float on the breeze out their screen door. Sadness left. Anger left. Need left.

She minded more not holding the children rather than dealing with the family gossip, so she put up with their assumptions. Not many people around Haida Gwaii were shy about handing their children over to her, though. It showed trust, really, a mother's trust. The little girl smelled sweet and a bit like sour milk. The mixture made Anna want to drink in her hair, her clothes, and her chubby neck.

With her free hand, Anna plucked a piece of salmon from the large ceramic dish. She had baked it this time, laying the fish out as foundation and pouring the marinade over it, also sweet and sour.

She did not like fish or seafood when she first came to the island. A bit of a problem if she was to eat, especially with Aaron's family. Fishing for their food meant survival and eating through winter.

The flake of salmon fell into her mouth, an old habit now. A slight aftertaste remained of salt and things of the Pacific Ocean and bays. The almost two-year-old reached out for the fish.

A flick of Anna's fingers grabbed another chunk for Lily, who stared at it. Then her tiny hands stuffed it in her mouth, teeth and lips and squeals of joy.

"Did Nana give you salmon? It's her favorite," said Nari. She took Lily into her arms. "Thanks for holding her."

Nana. A name she became a few years ago when grays traveled through her hair. She could never be a real nana, but liked the name just the same. And she guessed she could have been one by now, in another life.

Aaron watched his wife move through the family crowds, her motions dedicated to showing them a comfortable time. He saw Anna cling to these get-togethers. They roared with people and the vibrations of generations. And the bodies closed in on their small home. The lack of space didn't seem to matter if it was his family.

Her back would pull straight, like a cord was attached to it on either end. The bun of red light pinned, kept layers of hair in order. This order didn't mean detachment or an overcontrolled environment. She rolled with each thing as it came: running out of certain foods and replacing with others, spills, kid fights, animal fights, relatives that must be kept separate.

He wouldn't trade her or change her. So many had wondered why a white woman. He wondered why it mattered. But knew.

"She caught you, didn't she?" his sister Donna had said. She meant well and liked Anna. Things about people, things she didn't like, didn't ever truly dissipate, though. Not with her. His brothers slapped him on the back the first introduction and never thought twice about it again. Somehow, he figured it would be the opposite. His brothers followed tradition so strictly.

"Flighty," his sister had said then.

"Feisty," he wished he had said back.

A man whose face he only somewhat recognized pulled him away from staring at his wife, asking, "Aaron, what's the next project?"

"Mmmm, a totem pole."

"I'd love to see it."

"Park's admission will do it."

The man nodded. A little light left his eyes, as if an idea diminished somewhere.

Seeing meant talking—somehow revealing himself or his work and always the "why." Lately, he only wanted to get to work, in and out. He politely talked himself away and into the kitchen. Maybe that was a mean response. Sometimes he couldn't let go of the anger.

"It's amazing what Anna can do with salads," Donna said. She began filling emptied bowls with new food items. "She's doing well with *this*." Her free hand waved around the room. Blue-corn chips hit with a clatter. Tuna salad slid into another bowl.

He nodded. Anna did well with each party. Rain or sun.

Once his sister had said, "It just . . . didn't seem like she came back a whole person after her mother died."

It showed in Donna's eyes now and again, some kind of concern mixed with judgment. Anna did lose energy. The weight deflated her questions, her movements, her words. She shifted into a quiet realm where she took more in with her eyes rather than her mouth. Some of it came slowly back. He saw it at these parties, and in her weaving.

"Here, take Lily, Mom," said Nari. She shadowed the doorway, handing her daughter to Donna. Her voice was not as high as his sister's. And she seemed to have a consistent smile since Lily arrived.

Donna walked away, cooing in the little girl's ear. She pointed outside, showing her the birds and trees, naming them.

"She talked to you like that," he said.

"Hey, Uncle." His niece hugged him and kissed him on

the cheek. "I've been thinking, you should give Lily carving lessons."

"She's a bit young."

"And female." Nari laughed. "She likes hanging out here. And she just stares at anything you make. Never looks away."

"Maybe we could. Maybe."

Anna came into the kitchen, picked up a few bowls, and headed back out with a slight nod and twinkle. His heart skipped. It still did that when she flirted.

They could see Anna through the doorway. She flipped a piece of hair behind her ear and put a hand on his great aunt's arm to steady her.

"She's good at these things," said Nari. "This many people drive me batty. Andrew knows I try. But I run around like a crazy woman waiting for the next disaster. You'd think I would be used to it with everything our family does." She turned to him. "I know Mom's not nice sometimes."

Aaron played with a pencil in his hand.

"I didn't know Auntie before . . . but she was always kind." His niece took the pencil from him, which he had begun to doodle with. "I detested myself in high school . . . I liked pushing people away." She fiddled with the pencil, tapping it against the counter. "She kept talking to me anyway. Saying I was good and special. It sunk in after a while." Nari paused and looked out the window at her mother and daughter.

When Anna hadn't come back after her mother's stroke, rumors traveled quietly through the village. They expected him to go after her, help, then return with her. When that didn't occur, they made their own assumptions. She stayed back in her world, they said, because that was comfortable—somehow right. She surprised them when she came back. But not

Aaron. However, he couldn't ever figure out why he didn't go to her, even against her wishes. He wasn't there for her when she needed him most.

He and Anna didn't talk about her previous life after they married. Her family existed in country clubs and on yachts. Not in their lives. And Anna was okay with that. Now he wondered if he still was all right with her silence.

"I'd say she was meant to come back." Nari gestured around the room and pointed at him. She squeezed his shoulder and handed the pencil back to him. "Well, we've got to go."

He doodled more on a napkin after she left—a tiny sketch of a small sea monster.

Other guests began to disappear with the afternoon light. The house grew quiet again, calm.

He took his wife by the hands once the last person had left and led her into the living room. She didn't protest. With his hand cupped in hers, they stared at the fire.

"I always like this," Aaron said. "How it gets quiet."

"Don't you miss the whir of people?"

"No."

He kissed her.

The fire lit them in orange and yellow.

Anna sat on a stool bent toward her weaving. The strings lay between both sets of fingers. The pain in her lower back and shoulders felt dull. She had been arching her back this way so long she forgot the pain as she wrapped the strings of yarn rolled with cedar bark just so.

Her eyes occasionally grazed the design board Aaron had painted. But she knew it, went over it with him months ago. She talked him out of drawing Mouse Woman this time. You could not see one of the animals without recognizing body sections of the other. One became part of the other.

"Why not move this here and here?" She used Aaron's pencil like a pointer. Years sitting together meant things rolled off her tongue easier. "And thicken this line here, by the monster's head."

She could see a sketch, let it float through her mind, and point out changes for curves. It was something like how she saw the design as she weaved it. One existed in her fingers and the other in her mind. She drew her own sketches in college and then painted some of them.

The women don't design. She respected that now, but still didn't quite understand it. It was solely always done that way.

"These are good suggestions," said Aaron.

He used to cringe at them, as if her words sounded unnatural or garish. She touched his hand. "Thank you." She held back this urge to say more, sketch over things, erase. She knew his process took him deep into himself and his ancestors. Sometimes she felt the itch in her own fingertips—different from weaving, but the same—a kind of flow in the blood.

He erased some of the lines and shifted the design a little in Anna's way, still keeping his own traditional way, too.

With each addition and change, she memorized the workings of the design and pictured them becoming strings moving through her fingers. It became habit after so many years.

"I think I'm done taking on students." Anna even surprised herself when she said it. The reaction she expected from Aaron didn't come.

"Are you sure?" he said.

She nodded.

She wanted to get her blankets done. It wasn't that she

lacked the duty to weave. She learned it, then felt it fly in her fingers, almost like a need. The design becoming part of the thread through her. But she wasn't like Aaron. She didn't have the urge to pass it down. It may have been given to her by her teachers, but she lacked the history and it seemed a family connection. It simply wasn't the same for her.

When she died, what would be left were her hair combs, a diary in her large cursive with penciled sketches, a tidy house, and clothes lingering in lilac perfume.

"Okay." He leaned over and placed his hand on her back between her shoulder blades. His fingers pulled at the knot in her muscles. The touch felt light, but gave relief. A familiar movement that held quiet patterns between the two.

Her desire to stop teaching came from tiring of explaining. What weaving and teaching meant to her seemed like it was different for others. Maybe it was more ingrained in how they grew up. But the questions persisted in polite ways, of course. This generation asked a lot. Aaron had more patience with them. Teaching scarcely built the same excitement with her any longer.

As she wove, the black-and-red lines became clearer. To the naked eye simply looking at the loom early in the process, the purpose could remain a mystery. One twist at a time built a gradual picture. This blanket neared completion.

Aaron knelt on his wallboard—carvings almost complete. His knees ached. He kept this from his face and body movements. The light shone heavy on the place he carved. Sweat dripped from his forehead and underarms. The adz he held was his father's. Their finger marks filled the round handle with tiny indentations.

Because it was the middle of the island's summer, it also meant heavy tourist season, and a large crowd of people who knew nothing about Haida art or totem poles. They flanked every bit of space in the workshop.

Their breaths were obvious, their coughs, camera snaps, foot twitching, even the children rolling their eyes. Thankfully, the tour guide spoke for him.

He knew he could not gain studio space like this elsewhere. And he liked the idea of people learning something new and outside of their own comfort. Or at least he used to. Still, the tourists annoyed him with their incessant questions: What does that bear mean? What's a crest? What's that totem pole's story? Why did you choose that?

As if totem poles had answers. But it is the outsider way . . . to question. Maybe someday, he thought, they would learn enough from them not to have their questions.

He looked forward to those days, once or twice a year, when people actually understood—had studied the art before visiting. And he thought, too, about his wife. He worked the adz into the wood. Chips fell to the floor in small ripples. Her questions in the beginning had amused him, before too many tourist questions tired him. She still asked. But now she also voiced her thoughts. And not all at once—over time. Anna dug deep into the carving and into what he stood for. She made him think about it.

"Why this curve here?" she asked.

Or, "You know, the way these lines move together, they swell into the wood, like the ocean."

And the previous week, "Your work is darker lately, with deeper edges and colors that bleed into the wood."

He never questioned his carving or his pure connection to

the wood. He was just good at it. It simply came to him, lines curving along his brain.

He pulled out of this when there was a question the tour guide passed on. "Well, maybe our artist should answer that."

He questioned when the tour guide used that label. Artist. Historian. Carver, maybe. Art was never the original purpose of it all—not art like Europeans saw it, something to collect.

"What's that thing in your hand?" asked a kid who popped a bubble with his gum.

Aaron lifted his eyebrow and then said, "An adz." He demonstrated how he plucked and plucked at the wood, grooving it by chipping the wood away. Red cedar fell to the ground when he brushed it. More ripples. At least a child this age had time to learn—a reason to not know.

And more questions. Questions and interruptions. He would work late that night.

Anna ran her fingers over the grooves. She preferred the feel of the wood before the paint spread across the design. The smooth, soft touch reminded her of an antique bench her father once bought at a house sale. It had been worn by many bodies arching into the back of the oak.

Aaron's time and hands smoothed this wood. Anna's eyes traced the pattern back and forth over the crescents and U shapes. They leaped off the wood. Her favorite part of viewing his carvings was figuring out the forms and why he chose them for that wood or that commission. Sometimes her own designs became inspired from this—rolling in her head. But she never sketched them in front of him. A few made it into her journal.

Anna guessed at the designs when he finished. Most times, right.

Art. That was how she saw the whole process. He didn't. But no one else could create what he did. No one else could turn the wood out in that same way. These were not the patterns of his ancestors. They differed. They became Aaron, or whatever it seemed at the time he needed to channel in the grains. Some leaned deeper into the wood. Some sat high. Some patterns were simpler and more spacious. Happiness. Anger. Grief. Passion. It all came through the cedar planks.

Anna placed her hand on his shoulder and traced lines back and forth, rotating muscles as she went.

"Maybe it's time," she said.

"No." He closed one eye and stared at the side of the pole. Then he chipped in one spot with an upswept detail, a tiny tool for the details. His fingers stiffened, so he wiggled them, then twisted his thumbs in his suspenders.

"It's almost there, I think."

He had been saying that for two months about this piece. And he had slowed as the months moved forward. Commissioners gave them more time this year.

She dipped a brush into the black paint, tapped it on the side and swept it over his penciled design. This back arch was wider, and her arms stretched with the gesture. Now and again she might also tool away pieces of excess wood.

For some reason, he either avoided this particular pole or didn't have the energy. She couldn't tell this time. He strayed to different projects, like the now-finished wallboard, and then maybe moved back. What she did know was that he didn't talk about the arrangements made with the commissioners. He rarely angered or let it fall into his voice. But one phone call she overheard in snippets revealed maybe enough. No words, just tone.

The lines in this pole grooved more simply than his normal marks.

"What's this one for?" Anna asked.

"A totem pole park." He continued to chip away at the tiny edges, one eye careful on the tool, one eye cautiously navigating the design.

She waited a few minutes. The outdoor paint dried, and she moved the brush over it a second time, darkening the black lines again and again.

"So, it's a replication?"

"Sort of."

The designs changed sometimes from an original pole that had deteriorated, from one to another, usually navigated by the commissioner's desires and aesthetics, as well as the original pole's design.

"It's like a zoo, the way they're on display," Anna said. She didn't look up from the brushing.

"Almost like we're endangered animals," he replied. She was surprised he said it at all. He tried to quietly work in that world.

"Mmmm."

More paint dried. And more time elapsed. They had a momentum like this when she was between projects, her blanket or robe done, and he finishing. Except this pole was not even close to complete. She thought if he saw the black paint, he might work on the surfaces still yet to be carved.

"Art has to decay sometime," Anna said. "The poles that still stand 'saved' from the elements, we need to let them go."

"We didn't choose that."

"I know you didn't. But you could choose to retire. Maybe we could go stay in Sitka for a while with your cousin Bill."

"Shit, Anna. I hate this. I'm tired of the commissions and

the games. I want carving to be beyond this. No . . . *before* this way outsiders brought in."

His thoughts usually carried in the loudness of the silence—in what was missing versus what he said. In how he moved along the wood. Maybe all these years remaining quiet had built up.

"So, stop."

He sighed. "I still need to finish." He didn't look at her. Instead, his eyes remained on the smallest part of the design.

She was aware they might never leave Haida Gwaii again. She had learned to be okay with that. Sometimes more than him.

A knock on the window in the back of the shop drew her eyes. Aaron didn't notice. Some man gestured to come inside. The museum was closed. Usually that meant quiet enough for Aaron to finish. She motioned him to go away. The outline of his body disappeared into the trees. Right now, she could feel that Aaron needed less people in order to dig into the wood. He shifted like this sometimes and could block the world away. But he would come back.

She watched Aaron move along the wood, his hands flying down the grains marked in lead.

He chipped at the totem pole. It echoed as the only sound in the shop. Anna had left earlier to make dinner. This was a slow carving. He hated not finishing, but he also had a distaste for this project. Commissioners now stopped listening to him and respecting his ideas.

He used the adz as his guide and something like a punching bag. He pushed into the wood grain and the lift of it vibrated up his arm. It didn't stop Aaron from holding back, though.

He did not like this design, how his pencil and paint marks launched around the trunk.

The slam of the shop door stopped him. John, his nephew, walked in, no knock. Aaron and his family rarely saw John. He had attended college in New York City and stayed there. Family gatherings never pulled him back. This didn't shock Aaron, as John had rarely attended them once he became a teenager. He seemed to sit on the outside. A disconnect put up by him that no one could figure out.

"Uncle," John said. He shook Aaron's hand and stepped back. His eyes floated along the totem pole, black pupils steady. "This your next piece?"

"Yeah. It's getting there." Aaron picked up a smaller adz. "It's good to see you."

"Long time. I know." His nephew stood by three long rods that held Aaron's many tools. A pristine row held his many versions of an adz. John picked one up, then another. He swung them at the wood, but didn't hit anything.

"You here to see your dad?"

"Yes." John remained by the tools as Aaron moved up the totem pole. "He brought me out here telling me it was important. Something to do with his health."

"Mmmm."

"All he did when I got here was talk about our family and how our family's declining. I told him, 'We're not disappearing Indians, Dad.' But he kept going on one of his rants. You know."

"I do know, ya. I think his point is that you are family, but you don't act like family."

"It's the same as when I was here. I still talk to Mom and Dad and everyone else."

"Ya, that is about all you did when you were here. But are

you talking *to* them or *at* them?" Aaron chipped away more wood. He could feel the vibrations move through his voice. He tried not to think about John. He had thought when the boy was born that he would be the next family carver. John had even grabbed people's fingers tightly—a good, solid carver's grip. He knew that things changed and evolved. But the older his bones, the harder it was to accept how the younger ones grew up with different ideas. Ideas he worried might interrupt their ways. Maybe that was why he didn't stop carving.

"I see." John's back stiffened at Aaron's words. "But there's no real health issues with Dad, right?"

"None that I'm aware. He probably doesn't know how else to get you here."

John stood still while Aaron worked at one spot. The wood seemed tough getting the one curve he tried there.

John cleared his throat. "Uncle, I have a few colleagues in New York who are interested in your work."

"Oh. Who?"

"Some from museums. One is planning a new art center."

"Art center?"

"Yes. Today's traditional artists and contemporary Native artists."

"You a broker, John?"

"I only thought I could send some business your way." John's face turned red.

John's body—his entire body—appeared annoyed, from eyebrows to stiff back. Aaron scanned the room. A few more projects lay scattered on the floor. And then there were those commissioned still in his sketch pad. He rolled his eyes to the ceiling a moment, then back to his nephew.

"I think I'm good, John."

"Oh come on, Uncle. It could be good for you and Aunt Anna. A nicer house. Maybe retire in a few years. They pay quite well."

"No. I've got enough. And Anna doesn't need more to clean."

"Who is going to take care of both of you when you get older?" John clanked the adz back on the bar. "This money could do that."

Aaron stopped his work. He swung the adz down hard enough for one last chip. Then he peered into his nephew's eyes. It was difficult to experience the emptiness that invaded the dark irises.

"Family, John. Family will care for family."

"Okay, Uncle. They will move on to others, you know."

"Fine."

John left. The shop door closed behind him with one last thud. Aaron paused for a few minutes before returning to the totem pole.

Anna drank her tea, a few sips here, a few sips there. She felt invested in the morning when completing the ritual. The small kitchen left room for a two-person table. But mornings were hers here, with a steady gaze out the window. The Haida Gwaii mountain range, snowcapped, created sheer walls that rose out of the ground, with grass and flowers and tree roots defying gravity. Craggy rocks held deep gashes like layered scars left by the backhoes and dynamite.

The butterflies, wings opening and closing with a rapid flutter, remained her favorite. She could watch them as long as Aaron could watch his eagles.

A raven's croak steered her eyes away from the yellow wings. Crazy birds, always mucking about near anything scavengeable—her berries this time.

The doorbell interrupted the next sip.

"Nari," Anna said. She hugged and kissed the young woman. During high school, she was hard to speak to. But she saw light deep in her eyes that some people had missed back then.

"Auntie." Lily in her arms barred the hug from a whole embrace. But the squeeze held tight.

"Lily wanted to see Uncle. She pointed at his picture this morning."

Anna raised an eyebrow. "She's a smart one. He's out in the shop. He'll probably be there until dinner time."

"Ah. We should go catch him then." She uncramped Lily's hands from Anna's hair. Hands that somehow strayed during their conversation. "Sorry."

Anna shrugged. She liked the feel of the little fingers gripping tightly.

"I'm leaving Lily there for a bit. Could I come over and watch you weave?"

"I haven't gotten to weaving this one yet," Anna said. "I've still got more wool and cedar to roll."

"Then I'll come over and help."

Anna nodded.

By now the tea had lost its steam and some flavor. She microwaved it and sat by the loom. She pulled the wool out and let the cedar strips drip off some of their water. Then she rolled the two together on her upper thigh. The strength of the string still amazed her.

Nari had never asked to work with her before. No one in

their family had. She had learned by asking the same way. But there weren't weavers in Aaron's family. She traveled to be taught in their community and further south. Sometimes she had to drive far or take a ferry to learn. Aaron encouraged it after her mother died.

Aaron hadn't painted the design board yet. But the sketch lay across the board. He hadn't shown her this one. And frankly, something seemed off about it. She kept rolling, creating a rhythmic movement in the process. She wanted something different from the weaving.

The wool and cedar gathered together almost like one. Their colors gave them away. White against khaki. Strings piled next to her. She found that once she got going, she could roll for hours until dizzy. The only thing stopping her this time was the doorbell and Nari returning.

Aaron looked up in time to see arms wrapping around his neck. The heft of Lily entered his arms as he took her from Nari. "Well, a little visitor."

"Yes. Upon her request." Nari paced the workshop—touching a tool at times. He noted her glances while he carried her. Lily gestured to the totem pole and he leaned her over the carved portion. She picked up a tiny adz and swung it around.

"Oh no. Not a toy." He pulled it out of her tight grip. "Let's not smash an eye, here. Ya."

He chipped at the excess pieces of the pole with the small tool. As his hands flicked at the cedar, his voice carried directions. Step by step, he crooned to Lily. He never heard Nari leave. Lily's eyes remained on him, and she felt the carvings as he explained them, her little fingers dipping below the grooves and following the forms.

Aaron sat by the large trunk of wood and ran his hands over the smoothed and readied surface. The shop was empty again, Lily eating dinner with her parents. The sketchbook next to him held many things he never got to. One in particular remained on his mind, one from the day he met his wife, set down and unfinished.

He picked up a pencil and began outlining. His eyes moved to the high ceiling and the beams cutting across the peak. Back down his eyes rested on the page.

The commissioned totem pole lay next to it—unfinished.

"Tell them," Anna had said to him last week. "Tell them you're done." If he could, he would return to it. He kept his word. But the things that came first needed to change, as much as the wood carved became something more than a tree.

As Anna headed into the kitchen to put water on, she passed the design board with Aaron's lines for her next Chilkat blanket. The lead lines remained yet unpainted.

With the steaming water pouring into the mug, her thoughts continued to wander to the design. It stopped her when she passed the room again. Tea and mug now down on the bench in her space, she picked up paint and paint brushes, hovering over the design. The pause was momentary. Bristles met the cedar board as she changed the design—lines thicker, figures swirling into one another.

The kitchen doorknob jiggled and the door opened.

"Nana!" Lily thumped her shoes as she ran in. She stopped to watch Anna.

Anna nodded at her and recognized a light in the small child's eyes that emanated from her own eyes when she was young.

Aaron came in behind Anna and stood at the back of the room. The picture of Lily tilting her head toward the wallboard and Anna intense on the design reminded him of when Anna used to paint. She lost herself in the images and often remained at an easel until she finished. He missed that part of her.

It was a good design. Maybe better than his original one. He touched her hand with his, gently. She paused and they met eyes, each one smiling.

Aaron pointed to one area she had already revised. "What about a *U* shape here?"

Anna pulled herself close, peered at the image, nodded, and then rounded the figure. She thickened certain lines, too. The warmth of Aaron's hand settled into her back as she continued drawing, fingers flying along the wood.

Calling the Ancestors

He stands along the edge, the outside of the crowd, praying. He bows his head, eyes closed. Beneath his eyelids, a maroon shade appears. Flashes, images, pass each other, his mind creating them from his past, sometimes perhaps his future. Now and again his mouth moves, forming words he knows and some he doesn't know.

The wind blows his hair behind him, cooling his neck and back. The sun is setting, but still July warm. In Victor, New York, eighty degrees easily feels like an Arizona ninety, even though they stand stretched far from Rochester's city buildings. Decades have passed, his time away from home.

He searches his mind. Hunts and waits for more words to come. He knows the songs, all of them. They beat through his blood, even if he hasn't learned them from his grandfather or sung them with others. He can call them forward.

A young woman explains this to the children as they wait, ready to learn. Her soft voice carries. We need to wait for him to find the songs for today, she says.

Songs he had sung appear in his consciousness, another man singing them. He hears but doesn't see the words. The language he learns as he sings and as they sing to him when he closes his eyes.

You cannot learn without them, his grandfather had told him. They hold our traditions, just there. He holds his hand above his head, then touches his heart. It will connect here if we listen.

So he listens.

Certain images, he wonders if they were from the past, not his past. His family's past. They are not his future, that he can tell. Strange clothes and familiar strangers.

He shakes his head, keeping his eyes closed. He clears his mind, stops the voices, and blocks out the people around him. A breeze blows again that his skin cannot ignore. He allows the leaves rustling, the grass touching his sandaled feet, the fresh blooms, all to come to him.

New words fall forward, enter his brain, and translates where he understands the meaning, but cannot make English words from them. He sways with the music, bobs his head, taps his leg.

Then another.

Old songs. From so long ago he can't place them.

Friendship. Brotherhood. A general sweep of deeper intentions and connections.

Words spill forth, and with eyes still closed, he sings quietly. This is enough to gauge tone, speed, and notes.

After twice through each one, he opens his eyes. Light makes him blink a few times. His visions lessen, although he still senses the earth below him, holding him up.

He hands a few boys their own small drums or rattles.

He begins to sing, his voice soft, then increasing in volume and intensity. The boys dance behind the men, their shuffles smaller, him stretching his stride, his voice gaining strength. He first sings the songs he knows, ones only for the men who circle with him.

Waving her hand, the young woman encourages the children and even some new adults to join. The men dance first during the men's song and then there is a song for all, she describes.

A small boy, maybe three, tries the steps. His feet not quite big enough and his body not quite tall enough to carry a beat. But he tries and almost copies his uncle in front of him. The boy does not take his eyes off his uncle's feet.

Even singing and pulling songs, he notices these things. How each dancer moves, their steps communal, but their own. No two alike. Some more confident and hard stepping. Some softer, careful. Cautious. New at this.

He joins the dances for this. The lessons. What his grandfather had given him, he gives to them.

He steps and sings and drums. The tone vibrates through him and around the group, forming a small circle.

They all vibrate. He sees the movements through them, repeating the beat of their blood. All blood. Repeating the steps of hundreds of years. Today. Different. Always different. Yet always calling the ancestors, right there. With them.

Stomping together. Patting down the grass. Patting down the grass.

Nothing but Gray

The fall scents wove their way through the air. When leaves crumbled under Gabriella's feet, they gave off musk and dirt and damp grass. She loved the crinkle noise they made and the echoes of rakes scraping the ground to grab the leaves and sweep them into piles.

The house Gabriella rented with two roommates loomed large behind her, shadowing the walkway gray. Park Ave was full of these houses, all unique. She pulled mail from the box at the end of the drive and turned back. The white siding, black shutters, red brick foundation, and a front porch made it seem like a real home. Then there was the aqua-blue door that stood out along a street of black or brown doors. Mr. and Mrs. Sandala took care of the property and were good landlords. They regularly checked in on the girls, yet left them to their lives.

Although Craigslist was known for its creepy invaders, Gabriella somehow found both her roommates there. Stacy and Lucia had known each other since grade school, but lost touch after middle school. Only when they all met together to look at the apartment did Stacy and Lucia realize their past connection. It seemed to Gabriella an instant connection between the two—one she had not ever felt with friends or even with these two. But they all got along well. They found the house fit their personalities, warm, open, and comfortable.

Cinnamon and vanilla from Lucia's cookies hit her nostrils. Flipping through the mail revealed junk from car dealers and Medicaid. Clearly they paid no attention to age. She was only twenty-three. She pushed her auburn hair behind her ear and crossed her legs while standing. A very large red envelope addressed to her stood out. Her mother's handwriting scrawled Gabriella's name. She sent her cards for most any occasion, really anything to send a card. This was marked "Happy Fall." She simply signed it "Mom" with nothing else but the date. This was as per usual.

Another envelope, small and square, was also addressed to her. This writing appeared unfamiliar. Yet because of the handwritten address, she knew it was not junk mail.

The opened flap revealed an ivory card with a purple border—nothing else. Strange writing filled the page. Gabriella caught herself on the edge of the counter.

Dear Gabriella,

I'm your sister. It took some time to track you down. So the agency is sending this out. I know this is sudden. But I felt it was the right time. Our mother—your mother—believed we should leave you alone. "She has a new family," Mom would say.

Mom passed away two months ago. We've all been wanting to contact you. There are five of us all together. Me,

Nathan, Dee, Jeremy, and you. You came last. But that's a story for another time. We hoped you would come visit and learn about us and our Seneca background. Please come see us. We need to get to know you. We have for some time.

Please call me and let's set something up.

Love, your sister, Mia

She walked upstairs to her bedroom, all thoughts of fall gone. Even the ornate banister could not hold her up. Her vision clouded and cleared, clouded and cleared. On the bed, surrounded by large pillows, she remained until dusk darkened the walls and window.

Gabriella's parents had told her they adopted her—different ways for different ages. At three, "Mommy didn't grow you in her own tummy, another mommy did." At seven, "We love you the same. And we honor your parents who knew we needed you. You are a gift." At sixteen, "Sometimes, parents can't care for their children. Circumstances just don't allow it." Those were the only words, though, the only parts to the story.

As she grew older, she rarely thought about why, or about her birth parents.

Keys clinking in the door awoke her from the fuzzy spin. No one could miss how loudly the thick wooden door slammed.

"Hello," Stacy called out. A few minutes later her heels marked her climb to the second floor. "Hey, Gabbie." Stacy put her hand on her hips. "*Hey.*"

"Hey." She looked at Stacy and then back at the wall, not seeing either.

"You seem lost."

"I'm okay. Just tired."

"Oh, okay." Stacy's heels carried her into her own bedroom at the end of the long hallway. They lost their pitch after she closed her door.

Gabriella folded the card which had sat in her hand all afternoon back into its envelope and put it in her bureau drawer.

"So, you've been mopey the past few days," said Lucia. She handed Gabriella coffee and a homemade pumpkin-spice muffin. "Come on, tell me. I even put extra vanilla in your coffee today."

Gabriella sipped the hot liquid and let the sweet bean coat her throat. She smiled at Lucia.

"A few nights ago, Stacy found you. She told me—"

"Yeah." Gabriella put up her hand. She pulled bits off the muffin and chewed them slowly. Lucia topped off her coffee and waited without saying anything. Gabriella sifted through the contents of her purse until she found it. The square envelope was now marked with pen and mineral makeup. She had moved the letter from space to space, carrying it with her, yet not opening it again.

Lucia took the envelope and opened it. Gabriella watched her roommate's eyebrows move up and down, and her mouth purse and open. "Gabbie." She put her hand on Gabriella's. "What are you going to do?"

She shrugged. "I can't understand yet, I guess."

Lucia nodded. She passed her another muffin.

"These are good. As always." Leaves knocked on the window as small drafts blew their branches. She put the letter back in her purse. "Why now? It seems so . . . like the movies." She shook her head and sighed.

"Are you going to tell your parents?"

"No . . . Maybe. This could hurt them. I think they always dreaded me even asking about my birth parents. So I never did."

Lucia poured Gabriella's coffee in a travel mug. Gabriella slugged on her coat and grabbed the mug.

Sun in the fall felt like rays digging deeply into the skin—rays that had been hiding since the summer. Rochester, New York, had few sunny days to begin with, and the heat of it warmed the interior of Gabriella's little Honda. She wished the warmth would last longer than this one day.

That night, she walked through the door into Stacy hugging her. Gabriella put her hands on her hips. "Really, she told you?"

Stacy smiled. "Oh come on. You had to know that would happen." Stacy plopped onto the couch, enveloped by the incredibly soft cushions, and folded her legs.

Gabriella stood there. She detested that couch. No support. It was a Stacy buy long before they all roomed together.

"Are you curious?" asked Stacy.

Gabriella shrugged.

"You should go." Stacy's voice hit high notes. "I would go."

"She's dead. I'm not sure what there is to go for."

"Your sister. Your other family. Your culture."

Gabriella's head shot up at the last word. Her parents never shared this background with her—maybe they didn't know. She had nothing against Native Americans. She simply was not sure how she felt about *being* Native American. It didn't mean anything to her.

"If nothing else," Stacy continued, "go to get to know your sisters. My relationship with my sister, Charlotte, is great. At least since we haven't lived in the same house."

"Maybe."

Stacy nodded and bounced out to the kitchen. Gabriella heard pots clanging and the *clack clack clack* of the gas. *How on earth does that girl find the energy?*

Gabriella went up to her room and pulled the card out of her purse. She read it again. "Please come see us," stood out. "We need to get to know you."

"Need" versus "want" showed her a desire for connection. What *did* she want, though? She usually wanted connection. She even picked up people's energy. But upon reverse, others didn't always want to know her. So she blocked taking anything in from them.

She didn't have a bad feeling or something nagging her mind about the letter or the family—simply fog.

Gabriella moved her mouse over the "call with video" button and clicked. The Skype line beep-beeped, resonating vibrations much like she imagined phones did back when you had to call the operator.

"Gabriella," said her mom. Her mother's picture popped up after a small swirling timer. "How are you?"

Her dad stood behind her mom. He seemed to be puttering with something at the desk. The wet curls hanging in her mother's face and large silky overshirt indicated a recent swim.

She waved at her parents. "Enjoying Atlantis?"

"Ohhh," her mother moaned. Her hand moved to her heart, which usually meant she was too happy for words. "The warmth, the sand, the blue of the water. Someday, you should come here."

"Not sure I like the idea of paradise trumping real life."

"Someone's moody."

Gabriella shifted in her chair.

"So why the insistence on talking today, hon? And like this? It couldn't wait for a phone call later?"

Her mother, adoptive mother, the mother who raised her she guessed, preferred bluntness. "I received a letter a few days ago. From my sister, you know, my biological sister."

Her father turned around and peered down into the camera. Light fell across the screen, blurring her mother's image. She imagined her mother unflinching.

"Mia. Her name is Mia. She wants me to visit." Gabriella tilted the screen a bit for better light.

"That's great." Her mother's image returned. She sat next to her dad, their faces now equally sharing the screen side by side. Her dad nodded. The wallpaper behind him gleamed with sheen, as did the pillows around them.

"I'm still deciding if I will go."

Silence continued. While plucking a pen cap off and then snapping it back on with her thumb and fingers, her dad looked from her to her mother. Gabriella raised an eyebrow. Even through the screen, she felt the pressure—for themselves, for her.

"Did you know I was Native American?" She waited a moment.

"That was in your records, yes," said her mom.

"And you decided not to tell me?"

"Well, we didn't see the significance. There was so much going on during those first years . . . Will you go? To see her?"

"Them. I have four siblings."

"Oh. Them then."

Gabriella went silent.

Her parents waited. They said nothing. Her dad looked

down. He had a hard time with direct stares, which had always made her uncomfortable. How can someone not look some-one else in the eye? That also meant her mom spent the most time having the difficult teenage talks.

Her mother's answers made her very uncomfortable now, though. She couldn't place why.

"Yes, I think I will."

"Well . . . have fun. When do you leave?"

"Next week." Gabriella searched her mother's eyes and hands, the pockets of her mother's emotions. Nothing.

"Call us after?" Her mother leaned in. The light played with her face again, mottling her forehead and cheeks.

Gabriella nodded and waved. Her dad's wave back swung awkwardly.

The screen went blank.

She stared at it a few minutes longer.

Gripping a piece of paper in one hand and steering with the other, Gabriella curved the car, making turns down back roads as she followed the directions Mia texted her.

After pulling into the driveway, Gabriella sat in the car. She stared at the medium-sized tan house with a large lawn and low wooden fence. The trees lining the driveway stood in even rows marking the entrance. Large rolling hills flanked the backyard, a typical Canandaigua/Bloomfield landscape. It had taken her only forty-five minutes to get there. All along, they had literally been down the road from her.

She had not noted signs for the reservation and wondered if she was somewhere on one. Around her, trees dropped yellow leaves, blanketing the lawn. She popped the trunk and yanked out her small suitcase. She had somehow agreed to stay the weekend, even though they were so close. Mia insisted it would be easier with late events. So here she was. Lucia forced her into several long talks. Gabriella hadn't really wanted to come. Not once had she thought about the strangeness that would surround her.

Lucia tricked her with the darn muffins, though. They may have also changed her pants size, which she also did not appreciate.

Her palms grew damp and her underarms moist. Gabriella checked her makeup, dabbing her nose where her sunglasses had been. The makeup was almost gone from sweat.

A petite woman with an asymmetrical cropped haircut and long purple beaded earrings made her way down the front stairs to Gabriella's car.

"Hi," Mia said. Her nose and eyes were the same as Gabriella's, in shape and size.

"Hi." Gabriella touched her fingers to her nose.

The two stood next to the car. Mia surveyed her car and suitcase and smiled. Her hands folded in front of her stomach. The trees around the house framed her in that moment.

"Umm, well, it's good to meet you," said Gabriella.

Mia made a gesture as if she were about to wrap her arm around Gabriella for a hug, but then dropped her arm. *A hugger.* She shivered. Instead, Mia pulled up the handle of the suitcase and rolled the bag up the front walk. Gabriella followed.

There were neighboring houses set with enough space between. Each one was distinct in color and style, but most were a square shape similar to Mia's. Gabriella noted that here you were not looking into each other's windows. The designs were smart with the window placement and that much space separating them. Compared to her and her roommates' house, though, this was smaller inside and more modern.

Cookies were set out on the kitchen table with bottles of Ocean Spray juice. The cookies were the hard kind from the bulk bins at the grocery store.

"Why don't you settle into your room and come out for something to eat in a little while." Mia rolled the bag, and it bumped along the wooden floor to the back of the house. Bright colors with yellows worked across the middle covered the bed. The white cast-iron headboard curled along the wall.

"There are hangers in the wardrobe." Mia pointed to the tall furniture piece across from the bed, then pointed to the window. "That's the best view in the house, especially in fall." She paused. "Do you need anything?" Her voice rose on the last syllable and her hands shook slightly.

"No thanks."

She stood at the window after Mia closed the door. The afternoon sun lit the trees, igniting a fire of orange, red, and yellow. Greens appeared sharp in contrast to the colors. Trees and taller mums waved back and forth. She felt the floorboards' chill go through her socks.

Gabriella would have preferred to remain curled up on the bed, but she only stayed there a few minutes.

Mia set a mug with hot water in front of her. "We have peppermint, orange, Earl Grey, and cinnamon spice."

"Cinnamon spice," she said.

"Yeah, that's a good one for fall." Mia dunked a bag in and out of Gabriella's water and then let it go. "We decided not to overwhelm you today with everyone greeting you. They'll be here tonight for supper, though."

It was as if a cinnamon stick had been waved under Gabriella's nose. This was not one of those teas that fooled around with flavor. She picked up a cookie—a round one with sugar sprinkled on top. By its brown color, she assumed it would be molasses. When she bit into the cookie, it was difficult to chew. Hard did not fully describe its texture. And the molasses tasted more like cardboard and spices. She put the cookie down and sipped her tea.

"What do you do?" asked Mia.

"I work for the National Center for Missing and Exploited Children."

"Wow. Not-for-profit. That must be a tough job."

"It is. But finding them can make the month or the year. Amber Alerts help now."

"Huh. Good for you." Mia held a cranberry-pomegranate juice bottle over a glass. "Do you want juice, too?"

"Tea's fine."

"Jeremy teaches at Cornell University. He travels back and forth weekends during the semesters because his family lives here. He's in this weekend to meet you. Nathan's security at a publishing company, Thomson. Dee helps out at Ganondagan. And I'm an LPN over at Highland."

Gabriella nodded, but did not recognize some of the places Mia mentioned.

Mia dunked a chocolate-looking cookie into her tea. She caught the soaked pieces which fell off into her hand.

"Did you grow up here?" Gabriella pointed around the house.

"Not this house. My husband and I got it together. He's away at some farming conference. He'll be back tonight." Mia poured more hot water into her own tea cup. "We grew up on the rez and lived in a small trailer. Most of us moved off rez, though. Mom stayed there, until her last few months." She peered at Gabriella.

"This isn't the reservation?" Behind Mia, Gabriella could see the turning trees out the large window. Robins and sparrows had been flitting around the yard since she sat down.

Mia put her hand to her mouth and raised her eyebrows. Gabriella saw she tried to stifle a giggle. Her moving shoulders gave her away. "No, this is not the reservation. We're all going to a social tomorrow night. That way you can meet people. But that's also not on a reservation." She stood, picked up the teapot, and refilled it with water.

Gabriella could tell Mia was still laughing. *It was not that funny. Didn't some Indians live on reservations?*

Gabriella sat up in bed. She had lain down to rest for a few minutes. Looking at the clock, she realized she had dozed off for an hour. Butter and rising bread wafted in, as did deep voices and laughter.

She padded down the hallway, assuming they had begun dinner. When she heard her name, she stopped.

"She's nice. I haven't had a lot of time with her," said Mia.

"What did she say?" asked a deep male voice.

"Nothing much."

"Did she ask about Mom?" said a different female voice.

"No."

"Maybe she doesn't care," said the male voice.

"She's here," said Mia.

"That doesn't always mean anything." The male voice had gone cold and distant.

Gabriella tiptoed back to her room, opened the door, and closed it loudly. The voices stopped. She walked back down the hall, straightening her shoulders.

"Dinner's almost ready," Mia said. She smiled and gestured for Gabriella to sit at the head of the table. Settings were simple with plates, napkins, and silverware. Everything looked worn, but not terribly. Lived-in. A flower basket sat in the center; she believed they were mums. Much of the house was white with white farmhouse cupboards and molding. But blues and greens acted as accents. It was a bit mismatched.

The siblings introduced themselves. The male voice turned out to be Nathan. His handshake was warm and firm, but his wary smile distanced them. All together, Gabriella noted their darker skin, much more olive than hers. Except Mia's Charley. He was closest to her complexion. But nothing about them was what she expected to be Native, like turquoise jewelry or men with ponytails.

Mia brought out a fruit salad and one with beans, which she called "Three Sisters Salad." Then she carried out soup and a platter of chicken legs, wings, and breasts.

Gabriella took a little of each item and a chicken breast. The others heaped food onto their plates and filled their soup bowls. Food passed to the right, and sometimes across—no true pattern. Jeremy scraped his chair back.

"The bread," he said. He returned with a large loaf, glistening with butter and steaming. He handed it to Gabriella first.

"Thanks," she said.

He patted her hand as she held the plate and took a slice. His eyes held light which matched his smile.

The crust crunched, while the inside gave way to soft yeasty bread. Gabriella put her hand to her heart and nodded. No words came out, or needed to, as they all ate heartily. She truly did not know what to say. Who were these people? Only Jeremy had children, and Mia and Jeremy were the only married ones among them.

"Where did you grow up?" asked Dee. Pink streaks wound their way through a few strands of her hair. She played with them sometimes, twirling the pink in spirals on her finger.

Gabriella swallowed her bites of chicken. "Fairport."

"But that's right around the corner, practically." Dee's eyes became round and open. "How did we not cross paths?"

Gabriella shrugged.

"But shouldn't you have gone to festivals and powwows at least?" Dee's voice sounded shocked.

"No. Why would I?"

The siblings exchanged glances. Their bodies shifted in different ways. Gabriella could tell they were mirroring the same emotion, but she had no idea why.

Nathan's silverware made more noise against his plate as he flipped food into his mouth. He did not look at or talk to Gabriella throughout dinner. She wasn't sure what to make of him. But she recognized anger simmering, and it overflowed in his eyes when they didn't move.

Jeremy passed her more bread, and she took another large slice. His silver bracelet shined under the chandelier above them.

Their chatter both enveloped her and overwhelmed her. They had a way of talking that rang of those familiar with each other, those with a history. One might finish another's sentence or even a memory. Then someone else would start a conversation that clearly had begun another time. And the names, she could not keep up with all the names.

"Linn decided to put up a vendor table at the festival for next year," said Mia.

"It's about time. Her baskets will add something different from all the sweetgrass ones." Dee spooned more Three Sisters Salad onto her plate. "Did she talk to Janet?"

"Yeah. I'm not sure that went well."

"She has to learn to make nice. Janet can help her."

"Sam's cousin found that cave they've been looking for," said Jeremy.

"Yeah? About time," said Dee.

Jeremy nodded. "Some weird stuff in there."

Charley joined in here and there, but was the quietest among them. He simply sat back and listened, nodding. Mia touched his arm several times. Maybe that was how he was included.

Dessert was similar. Strawberries and their juice ladled over biscuits did not seem quite like fall. The sweet liquid slid down her throat. Someone mentioned a sacred fruit. Conversation rolled over her head. Any noise became just that. Noises she was not really deciphering. She could not keep up, and after an hour and half, she was exhausted. Her room and quilted bed sounded good. They hadn't even noticed that she slid out of the conversation. Maybe was never really even in it.

"We must be boring you," said Dee.

Gabriella shook her head no.

"It's getting late," said Mia.

They all rose from the table and began clearing the dishes and food—putting leftovers in multiple containers. Mia handed them out to each sibling as they left.

"Do you want some tea?" Mia asked.

"No, thank you," Gabriella said.

"Goodnight then." Mia put her hand on Gabriella's shoulder.

"Night," said Charley. His voice rang high.

Gabriella noticed Charley put an arm around Mia. It was not merely the typical arm-to-waist, but protective.

Mia took a step forward, then back.

Gabriella stepped away and walked back to her room.

Gabriella tossed around in her bed, getting tangled in the sheets. The wind made its way across the fields and hills, howling over the house. Or sometimes it sounded like whispers, as if it were human. All would become quiet, and there would be a voice.

She undid herself from the sheets and blankets and plunked her feet down on the floor. The wood pulsed cold into her veins. A light at the small desk in the corner haloed the area. She did not remember turning it on. A picture of her siblings stood at the corner of the desk, a deep wood frame surrounding it. They were children and standing in a bare yard. Quilt squares sat on the other corner. In the middle of the desk was a plastic brush, one of those you might have seen in the fifties or sixties. Brown hairs wove around the bristles.

Gabriella moved to the window and pushed the curtains aside. Everything lay in darkness. Shapes melted into one another. Gray cloud cover kept the moon from showering much light.

She heard whispers again, words, but nothing she could make clear. She thought she should be scared, but was not. Some feeling kept her safe. Blankets of black blocked any movement outside, if the whispers were in fact the wind. Still, she knew those sounds existed as words. They floated around spaces and corners, entering her ears, then flying out again.

Back in bed, Gabriella wrapped the sheets partially over her head, and she fell asleep to a voice which began to hum.

The crisp air bit Gabriella's nose and ears. She climbed into the passenger seat of Mia's car. The social was about half an hour away on 490. She didn't feel she could ask questions about the event. They even acted as if she should already know.

"You'll meet some of our cousins and friends." Mia switched her eyes from the road to Gabriella. Gabriella could tell from her faux cheeriness that she was concerned. Cars and large trucks with Wegmans or the *Democrat & Chronicle* scrawled across the side passed them on the left. The highway moved from trees to concrete and back to trees once they finally got off the exit.

She always liked the Park Ave and Eastman area. Ornate houses lined the streets along with oak and maple trees. Although the houses were quite different, they matched the largeness of the area, the history, and the wealth. Some were Victorian with turrets, some like her rental, large enough as if two families might fit, but they only ever held one family. Scattered around, there might be brighter colors on the houses themselves. But mostly, the landscaping served to brighten, while houses remained gray, cream, steel blue, or pale yellow. This time of year, the leaves' colors took over everything, covering sidewalks and lawns, while spindly branches waved in the air. The dusk falling across the sky lit everything in blue. No matter which part of the day, these streets remained in a quiet that only the cars' engines penetrated. It was like time held still there, even with the contemporary touches.

The Planetarium's parking lot appeared half-full. Mia parked in an open area away from the building, explaining,

"The large grapefruit trees by the Science Museum, at least that's what they appear to be, will drop their fruit onto the car in this breeze. It'll chip the paint." She opened the back driver's-side door and pulled out Wegmans bags filled with cakes and brownies she had made that afternoon. They sold them to raise money. "The socials are put on generally to help with some need. Tonight's money goes to the Cultural Center." Mia had explained this to Gabriella as she convinced her to mix the brownie batter. "Be sure you buy a raffle ticket or something. There's always great pieces someone donated."

But even while making brownies, Gabriella could not find conversation. Those moments were foreign to her. She was used to Lucia and Stacy's chatter filling spaces. In fact, they usually did most of the talking.

The domed white building emanating with light surprised her. The light filled the night as the sky darkened. She had only visited the Planetarium during the day a few times back when in college.

Once inside, they wound their way down a hall toward a gym, and Gabriella could hear a few voices. Outside the entrance, a table sat covered with pamphlets about things she had not heard of: White Corn Project, Native American Cultural Center, Dream Catcher Scholarship, and so on. The woman sitting there nodded at her.

The ceilings in the gym rose to heights covered in metal and fluorescent lights. Chairs and bleachers wound around the gym's walls, and a number of chairs stood in the middle. She noted what appeared to be a drum or two lying by those center chairs. Cakes, cookies, brownies, and pies sat on one table, and other tables held items with brown-paper lunch bags in front of them. "You put raffle tickets in the bags based on what you like. See anything?" asked a lady behind a table. A woman with long brown hair and dimples walked up and purchased an arm's length of tickets. Tearing the tickets off one by one, the woman dropped a few into a bag in front of a drawing of three women. Then she put a few more into another bag next to a large shirt with ribbons hanging from the front.

Gabriella sat down at the far corner. Crowds were making their way in. People stopped and talked to others at each step inside. She watched them laugh and lean in close to listen.

Dee entered the gym and waved at Gabriella. She talked to a few people as she made her way over. "You okay over here?"

"Yeah, fine."

"Join in. Check out the goodies."

Gabriella put her feet under her to stand.

"Dee," said an older woman. Gray bouncy hair enveloped her face. She hugged Dee.

"Regina," said Dee.

"How's that new sister of yours?"

Dee's eyebrows went up and her shoulders went down with her hands in her pockets.

"Oh." Regina looked at Gabriella. She held out her hand. "It's nice to meet you."

The woman's hands felt clammy.

"Everybody's curious. We're all happy you're back," said Dee. Gabriella leaned into her chair and pressed her back against the cushion.

The people milled about and filled spaces. Eventually a man picked up a microphone and asked people to take their seats. He greeted them in another language and then spoke what she thought he called the "Thanksgiving."

Men sat in the chairs in the middle of the room and picked

up drums and sticks. The music began, and other men lined up to dance. They all wore jeans, with some in tee shirts, some in flannel, and some in polos. The man at the microphone explained the dances as they went along. But Gabriella could not catch everything. When the women lined up behind the men, Dee nodded her over. She shook her head no.

People danced past her. It was not a slow movement, or truly fast. Colors blended though as she stared into the circle. The men drumming all swung their hands in unison, and a few opened their mouths wide to sing. Others closed their eyes.

The beat of the drum vibrated in her body and through the floor to her feet. Others seated around her nodded along, tapped their feet, or wrangled children, leaving no time for the beat. There must have been nearly a hundred people there already.

"It's a lot to take in," said a woman next to her. Gabriella had not noticed her before. Her long gray hair was streaked with darker gray, and her black eyes seemed so dark.

"Maria Jimerson," she said. She held out her hand.

Gabriella shook it. "Gabriella." She felt like shouting was necessary. Between the music and so many people, the sound pockets filled.

"Yes. I heard you were back."

Back? Why is everyone saying that? She had never been there to begin with. They were a confusing lot.

"You should join your brothers and sisters."

"No . . . Dancing was never my thing."

"It's not really about dancing. Though it is." Maria patted her hand on her knee to the beat and bounced her head along. "This one's the women's dance. Go. Go." She put her palm on Gabriella's arm and pushed.

Gabriella could not believe how strong the woman was. Dee saw her and her face beamed.

"Come on in." Dee took Gabriella's hand and pulled her behind her. "Watch my feet for a while. You'll pick it up."

Gabriella watched. Dee's feet shuffled. They moved back and forth without lifting fully off the ground. She tried to move in similar ways. She could not hear the beat that Dee seemed to glide in. Dee's whole body found the music and turned and bent and swayed. As they circled, people watched the dance. Gabriella kept misstepping and picking up her feet from the floor. Her body did not sway; it jerked. She noticed a few children pointing and some adults laughing, she was sure at her. Women dancing were smiling, maybe talking or laughing. Some women in the front showed serious faces without smiles. But they were not unhappy, more absorbed. Her head became light and images swirled, much like when she drank wine. They all merged.

She could not keep up.

The music kept going and going, with small breaks in between songs where they merely walked until one of the men began singing again. All she heard now, or rather felt, was the vibrations. None of this made sense. When one of the breaks came, Gabriella left the circle and left the gym. She wove through the hallway until finding the women's bathroom, and she almost fell over. She couldn't keep her balance.

Gabriella stood in one of the stalls, the door closed and her head leaning on it. Her body shook and tears rolled down her cheeks. She did not sob or curl into a ball. She simply let the tears come. No sound came out. She wanted to stop, to pull the tears back in. This was not her. None of this. So she held it all in, forcing her breaths in and out. A trick to get the tears to go away.

A few minutes later, Mia called out her name.

"Are you in here?"

"Yes." Gabriella dotted her forehead with toilet paper and wiped her face.

"Mom loved to dance," said Mia. "She said the dance lived in her feet and moved her each time the drummer drummed and the singer sang. I think the dance existed in more than just her feet."

Gabriella heard the sink turn on, water gliding down the white porcelain. The paper towel dispenser rolled out its brown paper with a squeal.

"Mom thought it was great when someone from the out-side tried a dance."

Mia's feet appeared under the stall door. She must have been right up to the door.

"We learn when we're little. It's so ingrained then. This must be hard for you." She waited. "The women's dance is one of the hardest . . . We're out in the hallway."

The door made its swinging sound, and then shut.

All of Gabriella's siblings and Charley stood outside the bathroom when she made her way out there minutes later.

"She looks tired," said Jeremy.

"We still need to ask," said Nathan. He folded his arms across his chest and leaned against the wall.

Dee threw Mia a look that Gabriella could not read.

"Didn't your parents teach you about us?" Nathan asked. His voice was steady and calm. But his face had grown stiff and his eyes black.

"No."

Her siblings held identical looks of disappointment.

"They didn't take you to powwows or festivals?" he asked.

"No." Gabriella shifted her feet, allowing her to stand taller.

"Did you ask them why?" Mia whispered the words. She stood out against the white wall behind her with her dark hair, olive skin, and blue top. She didn't let Charley touch her. Or he was staying away. Gabriella couldn't tell.

"No. We . . . No, I didn't ask because I didn't know. Why is the Native part so important?" Gabriella put her arms over her chest and held them close.

"What?" said Nathan. His face contorted, and she was sure he was upset.

Jeremy put his hand up to Nathan as if to hold him back. "Do you want to know about being Seneca?" he asked. "Do you want to know us?"

"Of course I want to know you."

"Give her time," said Mia. She reached out and placed her hand on Nathan's shoulder. He let her hold it there for a moment, but then walked back toward the gym. Mia remained, while the others followed him. Charley brushed her arm with the tips of his fingers.

"Are you overwhelmed?"

Gabriella nodded.

"I get it."

She backed toward the bathroom again.

"You need to know us. That's why I wrote to you." Mia placed her fingers together, intertwining them, and then pulling them apart. "But ultimately you have to make that decision. Here." She handed Gabriella her keys. "Take my car home if you like. I'll be back when the social is over."

Gabriella grabbed her coat from the rack and walked out.

Once back at the house, she passed the kitchen and headed to her bedroom.

The curtains waved in ripples from unknown drafts. They stood open. She had closed them before leaving. A gentle murmur floated into the room and sounded familiar. Gabriella pulled the curtains across their rod until they closed again, and she left the room.

A fireplace stood at the center wall of the living room. Around it hung pictures of people, presumably family. Gabriella stepped closer to them, leaning until she could make out facial expressions. One black-and-white photo of a woman, her back against a tree, drew her to its frame. The woman's eyes looked straight into the camera as if staring down life.

When Gabriella heard a car door slam that night, she put on hot water.

The front door lock turned, and then metal hit some kind of pottery. Mia pulled off her coat and tossed it across the couch. Charley took off his shoes. He headed upstairs, waving good-bye to Gabriella.

"It's getting cold at night now," said Mia.

"Tea?"

"That would be great."

The two sat down at the kitchen table, mugs in hand, blowing on the hot water.

"We just want you to feel at home," said Mia. She stirred a small amount of sugar into her tea. "Who's your family?"

"I have parents and a few aunts."

"We've got cousins and an aunt. But our mom, she was our main family."

Gabriella sat back and pushed her tea forward. She didn't

want to hear about her mom. She thought maybe she would. But she didn't.

Mia's eyes went dark. "Maybe it was too much all at once."

"You know, I had a good childhood."

"They promised us." Mia stared into her mug.

"I was fine."

"Mom only let you go knowing you would have both a better life and a good upbringing." Mia drank a few sips.

The wind blew outside, enough to scrape the windows.

Gabriella put her mug down again. The chamomile tea tasted too bitter. "My teachers and parents pushed me to be a better person, a good student."

"There were too many of us to make it all work in that trailer."

"We had a dog, Spots, when I was little," Gabriella said. "His chocolate-colored coat had one cream spot on the back. Don't ask me why his name was Spots and not Spot."

"We never had pets. Too much else to do. That's lucky."

Gabriella nodded. "I was lucky."

"She didn't let go easily."

"They loved me."

Both women dipped their tea bags in and out and then placed them on the plates Gabriella had set out.

Mia sipped her tea. Gabriella continued to blow on the water.

"Well, now you're here." Mia peered straight into Gabriella's eyes.

Gabriella stood up. "I think I'll go get some sleep." She didn't wait for Mia's response.

"That's Mom's room," Mia called after her. "You're sleeping in her room."

Gabriella's back stiffened.

In her bedroom, she sat on the quilt, running her fingers over the yellow sun shapes, and watched the moon cast yellow drifts of light along the yard and hills. Days grew less and less light filled. The voice whispered that night again. It traveled the room, becoming louder, then softer. Gabriella did not get up. As much as she tried, she could not decipher the words. She pulled up the covers and shimmied down under them, settling the layers to her chin. The humming began and lulled her to sleep again.

Gabriella rolled her suitcase out into the kitchen. It *thump-thump*ed over the ridges in the floor.

Mia had breakfast waiting: toast, hash, and eggs. She placed some of everything on a plate and set it out on the table.

"I'm not hungry," Gabriella said.

Mia picked the plate up and dumped its contents, returning them to pans. "You can always come back," she said.

Out the kitchen window, Gabriella could see the hills becoming pink in the early light.

"The light, it somehow filters out the harsh colors when it touches those hills," said Mia.

They walked to the front door together.

Gabriella turned to leave. She touched the doorknob, lightly, but enough to push open the door.

"Hang on."

Gabriella waited.

"Here." Mia handed her a square box. "She wrote you letters."

Gabriella took the box. It was heavier than she might have presumed.

"You know, she gave you that name," said Mia. "Mom wanted you to have a good American name. To fit in."

Gabriella did not look back at her sister.

"It means strength." Mia's voice broke on the last syllable. "Well, really, 'God is my strength.' Also American. But she wanted you to have strength, and so she gave you that strength."

The words entered Gabriella's ears. She took them in, but her feet carried her out of the house, down the steps, and to her car. She couldn't look at Mia. She just couldn't. Her body shivered, a reaction probably to the chill in the air. Leaves crunched under her feet. Fall was moving on. Blankets of snow crystals would soon cover the sidewalks and the grass and each tree branch.

She put the car in reverse and swerved around to face the driveway's edge. Her hand on the gear shift, she worked it over to drive and let her foot off the brake and hit the gas. She switched her eyes from the road to the rearview mirror. The house and the driveway and the large oaks in the front yard slid away from view, each one inching out of her mirror much like the end of a movie panning the camera out.

Then it was the road. Nothing but gray concrete and receding trees. She steered her car around a large curve, holding tight to the wheel and pushing down on the brakes. Rolling hills opened in front of her, dominating the landscape, and dipping her car in its changes.

Towpath Lines

Nebraska cold snaps against Carley's face as she steps out the door. The wind shifts and works its way over her body and through her hair. She pulls the door shut with the required yank and bang. Frigid air sucks in the noise and dissolves sound. When Carley turns around, dry brown grass lies like a worn carpet. Snow doesn't stay for long in the small city, although slices of ice and white drifts dot the hills and flats.

From behind the gray, the sun moves in front of the clouds and momentarily calms the wind. Carley rushes down the stairs to the parking lot. With each footfall, warmth spreads up her legs and she acclimates to the cold. She inches her hat further down over her ears. Today she walks left toward the bike path. Stretching her legs out as far as they will go, she climbs the hill to the pathway.

When squinting becomes the only method of seeing, Carley takes sunglasses out of her pocket. The round brown lenses make her look a bit Hollywood. Not that she wants to be Anne Hathaway or Kate Hudson. Not at all. But the glasses match her choppy haircut. And she loves how her long brown hair swings over her back and glistens in the light.

The half-orange ball in the sky heats up her wool-wrapped scalp—resulting in one extraordinarily warm body part, and chills tugging the rest of her body. She picks up speed and creates more leg tension, mostly to forget her single status. The burn means no cottage-cheese thighs. Her frame stands an average silhouette that follows behind while she strides past each yellow dotted line.

This path runs parallel to her apartment. It cuts through Lincoln's center, but continues far enough away from downtown to be green (at least in the summer) and lined with trees. The light dims in and out as Carley passes the trees and two-story houses. Even though it's winter and some trees stand bare, others still hold leaves in red and brown that cling to the spidery branches. She always thinks it funny that each house is surrounded by some kind of fence, either wood, green metal, or chain-link gray. She hasn't heard of robberies or property damage, unless a storm blows. Back east, fences usually line the larger, upscale properties or maybe a backyard if too close to neighbors. She doesn't always understand Nebraskans.

The path winds around a corner, clear and ice free. These bare areas appear weeks after sun's rays, which still never rid the air of breathtaking cold. People here walk these paths no matter the season, though. It may look like fall, but the bitter hurt cursing her throat speaks differently.

Fresh out of college, she gets a job offer at a hospital as a pediatric nurse. Night shifts. Great job, but she often wonders why the first offer has to be in the Midwest. She doesn't want to wait for openings.

"Mom, I need the job," she says before leaving.

"It's so far away . . . and so different."

"It will be okay." She touches her mom's arm. "Maybe there will be some kind of adventure to it." This is her first time living on her own.

"But your community is here."

That's partially why she moves. She wants something different from the smallness she feels in Rochester—like the city closes in on her because she knows the area so well. And everyone in her community knows her. Knows the hand-me-down ribbon shirts that are always too big. Knows the time she throws up all over the table during a feast.

Nebraskans being different is purely perspective. People are people. They are nice enough. Although the first time she sees the popular Huskers football shirt—"I SEE RED PEOPLE" in all caps—she balks. *Indians?* Turns out that "red people" are the red shirts on Saturdays. Crowds and crowds walk toward the stadium like a sea. But still. A large difference between Nebraska and Rochester is the weather, which this time of year creeps into her bones and they ache sometimes. At least it isn't tornado season. That scared the bejesus out of her in August. All those low-hanging clouds you can almost touch. She realizes then that if one came, she has nowhere to go that's a safe haven.

A girl with a large faux fur–lined hood nods at Carley. Carley smiles back. She notes her half-zipped black jacket, shoulder bag, and creamy skin that glows with youth. The girl, a young teen and probably barely leaving school.

Two bikers call out, "On the left." Their pants shimmer blue and hug their lines. Carley picks up her pace. Young male joggers run toward her with short sleeves and red cheeks. Heavy inhalations reveal their struggles breathing. The one nearest her turn up a dimpled smile. She catches his eye and returns a slow, deliberate smile.

"Hello," he says.

"Hi," she says.

He passes by, without a look back.

With school getting out, the rush to vacate anything school related quickens with the more teenage paces. A group of girls enter the pathway from the football field. They seem in their own world, their own time. Sometimes their gait slows, and they lean their heads in toward each other as if the secrets need to be kept alive with chatter.

In high school, Carley likes a lot of activities and has a few close friends. It's with those close friends that she remembers arching her head in the same way as these girls, laughing with the same pitch of giggle.

Raina calls her last week. Her one high school friend she still talks to. They talk often, but haven't seen each other since Carley moved there.

"We miss you here," says Raina. The "we" includes her husband, Shawn, a man Carley adores for Raina.

"I miss you, too."

"Come home soon."

After hanging up, she stands there staring at the glowing screen. When she finally lowers the phone to the coffee table, she notices the large darkening sky spreading out from her window to more horizon beyond. The apartment spreads out large and empty. This is home now. Making her own way. She wants it this way. But there's no "Raina" here yet.

Two tall, lanky boys stroll out of the trees and cross in front of her, her mental wanders disappearing. They keep their heads down and snicker. She can't tell if that's meant for her, or if they, too, hold private jokes.

Most people she sees on the path are what she calls "winged walkers." They speed walk with arms out flapping along with the beat of their sneakers. Calorie burn or not, Carley thinks it a ridiculous look. Today is no different. Two pass her all too quickly, one in neon purple, the other in gray.

Her knees grow tired, and needlelike points spike up and down them. The early signs of her family's osteoarthritis. Her doctor has told Carley that building muscle will help. Carley continues on. Pain doesn't stop her.

Her mother is on her second surgery this year. Deteriorated muscles from the arthritis has broken down her ligaments to almost nothing. Carley flies back, taking a few weeks off. Her mother doesn't stay down long. A spunky woman.

"It's just the knee, Carley," she says. She pushes her daughter away playfully. "I can pick up my own room. It's been you and me for so long." She touches Carley's face.

"Mom, you only got out two weeks ago."

"Those were some good physical therapy sessions."

"Was he cute?"

Her mother blushes. "Too young for me. But it helped." She laughs.

Carley watches her mother make her bed.

"Take me to the social tonight, Carley."

"Mom, are you ready for that?"

"We go when we can. Right?"

"Yeah. We do." Carley crosses her arms. "I'll be back for the holidays, you know."

"I know." Her mother holds Carley's arm. "It was good to

see you. And I love when you come home. I do believe you should be here. But . . . sometimes, they fly the nest." She pats her. "These feet need to dance, girl."

She dances for her mom that night, while her mom taps her feet.

Afternoon turns into early evening in minutes with shifts of cloud and a denseness in trees lining the way. Cold drifts under Carley's parka. She shoves her gloved hands deeper into her pockets. The stupid lining that protects from below-freezing weather doesn't do a thing for her numbing fingertips.

The thought occurs to her to turn back. But she has only been gone twenty minutes. She wants to walk an hour today. It's pointless to brave the cold for anything less. Carley's shivering causes her to stop and adjust her scarf and hat and draw up her hood. It was then that her head jerks up like a puppeteer tugging it on a string.

No one moves ahead of her. The path lies empty except for drifting leaves. Noises filter down from above. A squirrel sits on a branch *trr*ing at her. She has invaded his home. She laughs. That has to be it. *What weird sounds.* This squirrel's noises come from deep in the belly and vibrate along his brown fur. The tail arches with each guttural chirp.

"All right, I'll move," she says. She tries to stare into his eyes, but he peers over her head.

Carley's hair tingles along her arms. A shadow of birds in a misaligned *V* flies over and beyond her. None of them make a sound. The air smells of Bubble Yum. Watermelon.

The first blow hits her shoulder, knocking her to the trail. Yellow dotted paint fills her sight. Hands pull her arms back, straining her muscles to points she doesn't realize she has. Raw searing spreads an ill feeling through her stomach, throat, and head. Carley tries to kick, but a boot pushes into her back. The lines and bottom indentations of the boot imprint her skin.

She screams.

Fingers invade her mouth and grip her teeth. Her head arches back, too far. And then, the body bounces once to smack her face into the cement. Heat pervades her body. Metallic fills her nose and mouth. No voice escapes her. Fists beat into her back. Through eyes wet with tears, the skinny trees look like round stakes with small arms placed haphazardly. They don't sway or bend. The wind stops. She catches one glance from the side of the seemingly large body holding her. A big hood envelopes hair, and a bulky coat the body—one body.

Carley covers her face, elbows out like the wing walkers. With each hit, she fades further. She does this by choice. She wants her attacker to think she has passed out, or worse. Maybe playing dead like the dogs showing off tricks along the trail will really work. Some deep part of her wants to truly be dead, or almost dead. Sounds disappear. And except for the vibrations of the blows, consciousness also leaves her body. *Make it stop.* Blurred images float around her. Or more like she floats and doesn't see anything, doesn't want to see anything, simply floats.

When the fists cease their punches, hot breath runs across Carley's face. Her attacker spits on her. The warm liquid stays on her forehead. A bristle brushes on her cheek, not from dripping wet, but from something soft.

Carley hears the boots clomp away. She squeezes her eyes shut tighter and remains still. In that stillness, her frozen mind thaws and allows her to feel the throbbing radiating throughout her shaking form, up, then down. But that's all that makes it through.

For moments of time she cannot place, Carley lies on the ground. Increasing pain is over. But the event isn't. It replays across the receptors behind her closed eyelids. She relives different variations, which she tries to simultaneously stop.

She hears voices in the distance. Their timbres make her shift and roll, facing the trees. Above her, the call of the squirrel sound quieter this time, less deep. Carley pushes herself up. Shards of sunglasses fall from her parka. She dry-heaves multiple times. The pit in her chest hardens with a pain like a bad hiccup, only intense and powerful. She forces her nausea down with her thoughts and stands. Bitter vomit rises up, yet somehow stays down. Carley's will.

Carley checks her pockets. Her keys and ID are still there— the shattered glasses the only thing gone. Images in front of her throw lights and colors around her eyes, but she can't make out shapes or actual objects. She squints. The light hurts her eyes, so the gray concrete below her becomes her clarity.

A limp in her right leg slows her. She pulls her hat down close to her eyes and holds her hood down over her face. When the hood steadies, she hugs her stomach. The move causes her to gag. Carley can't look at anyone. Only laughter or footfall reveal people on the path. No one stops to ask questions. Maybe they don't notice the blood gushing from her face and left hand, or the torn clothes. Or maybe they assume she's some homeless person. *How could the regulars not see me?*

She doesn't understand.

Why would someone single her out for this? But that thought proves too much along with walking.

With her head down, she concentrates on her sneakers. Pink blurs into gray until she hits a path of cement with green markings. She stops long enough to see "Scttr or DIE" in curving spray paint.

Carley's eyes fog over and refocus on the path under her feet.

She tries to push the moment out of her mind, but remembers feminine features, a small nose, and high cheek bones. And then she realizes, *faux fur*, faux fur feels soft, like the attacker's hood.

Carley pushes everything in her mind back.

She limps home, head down, her average-framed shadow following her. The thought of any more walks numbs her brain. With the slam and shove of Carley's apartment door, she falls to the floor, lying on the chilly tiles, sobbing.

Crowding the Dark Spaces

The black of the cave flowed into the lightless unknown. The space around it seemed bare of anything but rock and clouds along the skyline. Green had almost disappeared where the pines stopped growing, but scraggy leaves and bushes pushed through thin cracks.

They each clicked the fasteners on their backpacks. The four boys looked serious, as if they were planning a drum session for powwow. Their heads cocked together, their fingers followed the map in her cousin's hands.

They understood those lines better than the words of the powwow song.

He had talked her into letting the others come. Most of the time, she could refuse their involvement. This time, her cousin didn't listen. They volunteered, no, more like forced their way on the trip. They liked the adventure of things off rez, but that was about it.

Her cousin insisted on figuring the whole thing out—where

to go, what gear to take, anticipation of the cave's extremes. But she already knew all that he'd mapped out. She could feel the lines, no map necessary.

Her father spelunked. Had all his life. Her mom didn't let her go with him when she was young. Then one day around ten years old, choices blew softly out the window. Her mom passed of cancer. The disease came from nowhere quickly. And it was up and go with her father. She and her dad found their rhythm, though it was hard with such a large absence. The weight of his hand on her shoulder lingered with the memory of him leaning close to her explaining safety rules, gear checks, and all that caves could hold.

"Pay attention to the lines in the rocks," he had said when she was eleven. "They tell you stories about the cave."

She would stare at the rocks, touch them, watch how her dad moved among them. He respected the caves and walked slowly, careful not to disturb things. And he memorized their details. "Remember that cave with the swirl marks by the opening, the air in there was different," he recalled. "I felt safe in that cave. We're always watched over. But there, things were close to us."

She somewhat knew what he meant. She felt the same, too, like when sometimes warmth or dampness wrapped her in among the rocks. The air held her there in those moments, steady and consistent. What she heard or felt was an atmosphere that let her get to know all of its tiny details. And she leaned into that, took everything in, watching, touching, listening, and feeling the space.

"You get that from your grandmother," he had said. "She could hear the trees and read what was coming. Weather.

People. Deaths. You hear the cave." Then, he would go right back into cave-exploring mode. "Check your water. Check the lights. Do they work?"

Her cousin snapped his fingers. "Hey. You ready?"

She pulled herself back. Nodded at him.

"Come get your stuff," he said.

His friends picked up their packs and lights and fell in line behind him. Their strides matched the swing of their arms, all from years of boyhood together. She tailed the rear.

Her dad had described the cave he spent his lifetime searching for, something from his dreams or his memories that her grandfather had passed on, too. Only he hadn't known what point or hilltop contained these memories. So he searched the landscapes of New York, Ohio, Pennsylvania, and Massachusetts and their mapped caves, and he walked other trails simply looking for caves. He told her these stories throughout her life until she had this same cave invading her own dreams. Now this opening and the lines in the trees below seemed familiar, with details emanating through remnants of his voice.

"You sure this is it?" her cousin asked as they first rounded the corner and the shadowed cave entrance appeared. "How do you even know?" He looked at her from the corner of his eye. She was familiar with his skepticism, especially of her. Maybe it was a competitive thing.

"Give me a moment," she said. She stood at the mouth of the cave. With her eyes, she followed the lines and crevices. The air hit her skin in soft drifts and air pulled her inside. Her whole body desired to go. And her whole body recognized those lines from her dreams, even the way her skin reacted. The smell outside was pine. But right there by the entrance, that pine mixed with what she thought was age. A staleness that hadn't seen light and that had held in all it knew and attached the knowledge to its stalactites. *This is the cave.* Explaining why seemed impossible. The knowing drifted there in her mind and body. She nodded to her cousin. "I know."

He raised his eyebrows. Her voice conveyed a confidence she didn't always show around him. His face remained serious, eyes deep brown, indicating his trust. He nodded back.

She took in a few deep breaths. *This had better be right.*

They shuffled into the cave's mouth. Her cousin and his friends turned on their head lamps. She hated those things and carried a flashlight instead.

"How you gonna grab on?" her cousin would say. He meant if suddenly things dropped off or fell. He seemed to be the apocalyptic one in the family.

Her father had let her figure out her own equipment as a teenager. "Whatever feels right," he had said.

She didn't turn on her flashlight. Not yet. Their lights flooded the space enough. She wanted to get used to the cave as it existed and feel her way through touch and how it rose and fell under her feet. If illuminated by lamp light, her pale skin stood out against the black walls like stars in the sky. That's why her cousin led the way. He knew her process.

"Here, you put the pack on like this." She showed her cousin how to put on the gear the first time they took him out. He was eleven and she thirteen. She clipped his carabiners on and checked the pack's contents. Her dad had purposely picked an easy cave, one they had explored together many times before. Even though her cousin acted gruff, she could see a small light of excitement and curiosity.

He didn't touch things and his gait was quick. But he

swiveled his head all around as they made their way into the shadows. Nothing seemed to spook him.

"He's a natural," her dad said.

Even though her cousin lived on the Tonawanda Reservation, and she in Rochester, he came to visit often in the summers. His father had died young from early onset diabetes. And her father and their other uncles took over that role as needed. When they were little, they even bunked together on their enclosed porch, so much cooler in the summer humidity than the old house. Stars hung in the sky on clear nights, streaming the porch with low light. She could never sleep if there was a full moon, yet her cousin slept no matter what with a soft snore. Before he fell asleep, they pointed out constellations, competing for who noticed the most.

It was no different in the caves once her cousin began spelunking with them. He had to be first, the lead who took care of the mapping, the one checking gear. She didn't care. But she smirked when she read the map better than he. Her dad thought it good that he showed such a drive for leadership.

"Let him find his way. You already know how to get around these places," said her dad. He was right. She went more by feel than maps—the tactile kind of feel, and the emotional kind of feel.

"Hey, look what's up ahead," her cousin had said.

A small trickle of water made its way down one wall. Her dad nodded at her and put his hand on her cousin's shoulder. Their dark olive skins matched as did the tilt of their heads. Neither moved. Her dad swirled his hands around the wall, feeling for its natural markings and getting quite damp in the process. Her cousin remained standing back. She touched the wall with her dad, her paler, smaller hand matching the splay of his fingers, side by side.

If nothing else, the guys were quiet, also finding their way by intense concentration. All that echoed along the walls were crumbling footsteps, shifting rocks, the occasional grunt, and someone's aluminum water bottle swinging against a backpack with a clang. The cave kept them in a fairly straight line that first half hour. Slowly, they descended. Such small elevation changes, it almost seemed they remained level.

After an hour, her cousin stopped so abruptly that the guys bumped into one another. She had hung back far enough to avoid collision. Her strides, small and careful, slowed her pace.

"What's the hold up, brah?" one friend asked.

"Something's not right," said her cousin. He twisted the map around. "It doesn't indicate on here that we'd be further below ground. But feel that air."

"You can't always go by maps," said another friend.

She wanted to agree, but remained silent.

They all paused, peering up, then down, then out toward the darkness ahead. Listening. That and touch was all you could do in the rocks and moisture and endless black and gray. She listened to the air moving around the empty spaces, sometimes hitting craggy masses. It sounded like slow breaths.

"Guess it's nothing," said her cousin. He waved his hands, inviting them onward.

She remained at the back, steps behind. With each step, rocks and silt pushed through, forming a floor that rarely seemed to run flat. When she ran her hands across the walls, their grooves and crevices made each one unique and even recognizable. She loved this about caves. The swirls in her fingertips passed across small lines of veins, smoothed edges, all dry. Nothing crumbled in her hands. The hot air now dotted her forehead in beads and in pockets under her arms. The guys wiped their foreheads with rags or bandanas. They slowed to her pace.

Her cousin stopped once more. This time, two openings stood in front of them. He tilted his head toward the left, then the right. He balanced himself by putting one leg forward and straightening his back. The floor was beginning to get even more unlevel.

"We'll check this one. You go in that one," he said. He pointed her toward the right tunnel. Alone. At least he trusted her to do this. She just wasn't sure she wanted the responsibility, even though she was so sure this was her dad's cave.

She nodded and worked her way in, rambling around the pockets of sudden raises in the floor. The darkness had an odd way of lightening and darkening depending on the texture of the rocks and her focus.

"This is an important place to our family," her dad echoed her grandfather.

She had met her grandfather but did not remember much about him. He smelled of vanilla pipe tobacco, which would haunt her later in the strangest places. She could walk into a store he had never been in and smell him, or at least someone who must have smoked the same tobacco. A hunt around the store never revealed the smell's origin.

Her grandfather told her dad many stories—Creation, family, his own life. One stood out to her dad that he took seriously. It seemed to connect to all of the other family stories. Each autumn, as things settled down, he relayed the story about a cave. A great-great-great-great-great-uncle had found his way there after hearing about it from yet another cousin. It contained something that either her grandfather couldn't, or wouldn't, explain.

Her grandfather's stories never told of the cave's exact location, merely what it held and what it looked like, surrounded by several tall, old pines that came to sharp top points, boulders all around, and these very specific lines. Lines that needed long periods to describe and dreams to see.

When her grandfather died, she was five. Her mother was still alive and consoled her father. It was the only time she saw him cry openly, deeply sobbing. He hid that when her mother died. She remembered him leaving so often and she wondering if he would even come home. Months after his father's death, her dad's search for the cave became more intense.

Now she suddenly dreamed of that cave and images revealed more details. Because she stood right by the cave in those dreams, she still didn't know its exact location.

She did internet searches and happened upon cave maps. Maybe this was her way, too, like him, of searching for her own dad among those rocks. Whenever she went in a cave, he was there again, part of her thoughts. She created a list of places that might have caves to explore over the summer and see if her cousin would join her. At the third map, she stopped. The layout of the cave seemed *familiar*. She absolutely knew—no explanation.

"That's the cave." This map, she trusted. Goose bumps ran along her arms, and her breath caught in her throat. She had trouble breathing and her hand didn't want to move the mouse to click on other maps.

Her cousin shook his head when she told him, but didn't

protest. Some semblance of light appeared for a brief moment in his eyes, though, a remembering.

"If we find it, we find parts of our family," her father would say. "There are connections in places that bring us back to our stories, and our heritage."

About ten minutes later, the walls around her crowded closer. Water tumbling over rocks in cascading force made its way to her ears, softly at first. It wasn't the normal dripping that many caves exuded down walls and across floors. Her flashlight reflected off of the dampness. As the water grew louder, more powerful, spray hit her forehead and the tops of her hands. A weight turned in on her shoulders, a weight she couldn't see, but knew was there.

She stopped before the water grew too loud. Leaning against the wall, layers of rock protruded into her back. They felt like support, though, rather than a bother.

All these years exploring caves, their eccentric characteristics were home.

Following behind her dad had never been easy. He had always liked a quicker pace, even though he explored caves like she did, feeling his way through. But he preferred light like her cousin. He would stop and wait for her when he wanted to tell her something or point out parts of the cave.

Then he would listen to the noises the cave emanated. "They have something to tell us. But we have to learn their language. It's a feeling instead of words. It's like our spirits that don't speak English; they speak our first language. And we can't explain why certain things are difficult to form into English words."

She didn't know much Seneca. Only the basic greetings. He didn't know much, either. When she grew older, she understood what he meant, though. She got easily frustrated with the other world, outside of Indian country. But it was the world she had been raised in. So it was hard to explain why she couldn't put into words her sheer anger at assumptions about her Nativeness. And why she couldn't describe how the caves talked to her dad and to her. They just did. And she couldn't express what the drums did to her blood and bones as singers called out the old songs. Her words fumbled trying to justify these knowings to others. Her cousin didn't get it, either. He tried to say the same thing about her not living on the rez, how she didn't understand. She walked away in those moments, wishing time rolled back to before her dad died.

"You can't always get those people there," her dad said. "They won't let the walls down to understand. They don't always know what's blocking them to connect with our ways."

Warm air curved its way over her face, not at all cooling. She unclipped her water bottle from her pack and swigged several gulps. She wanted to continue on, but the heavy feeling told her to turn back and find her cousin. Bring him back. The water faded somehow into the background, and what came to her ears instead were whispers. She didn't usually hear whispers that formed actual words. But those vibrations in her skin and mind, she knew them here. *Go back.*

It didn't take her as long to get back to her cousin and the boys. They had explored their side as well.

"What'd you find?" asked her cousin.

"We need to take that one." She pointed behind her.

"Why? We can feel air over in this one. We need to go further that direction."

She stared at her cousin. *Air?* "Why don't we at least try this way?"

He paused and thought about her urgency. Then his eyes blackened. She saw them often turn when something upset him, like mostly white teachers in rez colleges and Native wannabes.

"No."

The skinny one put his hand on her cousin's elbow. "Maybe she's got something."

She nodded. "There's something back that way. It pushed me to come get you." Her direct gaze at her cousin raised his eyebrow. He knew she meant come get him.

"You think it's your dad?" he asked.

"No." She really hadn't thought about it. Just something familiar. The entire cave held something to it . . .

"There aren't no Iroquois petroglyphs or even pictographs. You're looking for something your dad made up," he said. It came out quiet.

"Yeah, those are ghosts you need to forget," said his friend with the glasses. "We only came for the fun anyway."

The air in her lungs disappeared. Her head began to fill with a sharp heaviness. Her cousin knew the stories about the cave, and he had listened just as intently when they were six or seven, sitting on the couch with her dad. She figured that was why he spelunked with her when her dad died. Insisted on it. She had thought that he could remember those experiences with her and her dad in the caves and draw a connection to him.

But she threw back her shoulders and hid her sadness. "I'm going that way anyway."

The guys laughed. All but the skinny one. Hard laughs that drew up from the belly. The guy with glasses stopped though.

"That's just great, cuz. You go on and get lost in there."

On that summer porch under the stars, before she and her cousin fell asleep in those younger years, the stars seemed to conjure certain conversations. Her cousin was more open than usual those nights. He would tell the Creation Story. How Sky Woman found a hole in the clouds and looked down, down, until she fell and fell. The animals below saw her falling, and so they dove into the water surrounding Turtle. They were looking for mud to soften her fall. Finally, the muskrat came up with mud, barely in time for her to land. She danced around the back of Turtle, spreading the mud, shuffling and shuffling until earth was fully formed. Her favorite part was always the turtle as Mother Earth; how they were really all on the back of this huge turtle.

"So if we're on Turtle Island, does that make us really tiny or it really, really big?" she asked her cousin.

He smiled and replied, "We're all really small compared to everything we are a part of."

She thought she heard echoes of her dad's words in that reply. "So do you think, then, that dad's cave is real? Was Grandpa telling us something?"

"Of course," he said. "That's what our stories are for."

"What'll we find there?"

"I don't know. But it will be cool."

Their laughter followed her for a few minutes until the cave swallowed their hollowness. This time, she navigated the rises in the floor with ease as she made her way back to the water sounds. Nothing kept her from moving forward. And again, heat invaded the crevices of her body. She grew used to the heat as well as the space that continued to close in above and around her.

The beam of her flashlight revealed space opening up ahead. As her foot stepped forward into this space, she touched nothing. Before her momentum could pull her back, she felt herself fall, out into nothing. Instinct kicked in and she grabbed the wall and its little protruding ledges, the ones that had comforted her before in their sameness across caves.

She had to let go of the flashlight. It tumbled down into the nothing. The plastic split into small yellow pieces as it flipped over and over, until the light finally gave out.

"Shit." Usually she didn't speak. Something about the caverns and the dark made her go silent the deeper in she walked. Her heart flooded blood to her organs. It pummeled her rib cage. With her arms up above her and her legs splayed in awkward directions, she clung on like the wall was made for rock climbing. The bumps and divots were the usual ones, just larger in places. She didn't dare move. Her muscles were pulled to their limits, and she could feel a tug in one shoulder. If she moved, she risked not catching a hold. Eyes closed, she held her breath and reached out one hand.

She scrambled along until she found the ledge, her fingers and hands moving across the rocks as guides. She had never known what pitch-black meant until this moment. Light did not exist in this part of the cave—maybe it never had.

The walls felt of grooves and dips and sharp angles. Walking hands up the wall, she touched ceiling. Everything had become tighter, closer, warmer. Sweat trickled into every crevice as air turned to moisture.

The only sound came from the taps of her feet and hands and from another distant water source. She worried that she grew closer to water and couldn't see its depths. She had been afraid of heights a long time, since having nightmares about falling down a canyon. The place in her dreams looked like the Lower Falls at Letchworth State Park. But the grainy replay in her mind left her wondering each time.

This thought froze her. *Where are the other handholds?* She used her hands against the walls as if she were smoothing wallpaper. A flat surface with no protruding ledges. The same when she felt the wall with her feet. Sweat rolled down her forehead and into her eyes, where the salty wet stung. She tried to blink it away.

Her grip loosened. And she could feel the wind rushing past her, a scream lost in the caverns below. Her body floated among the rocks. The boys would never hear her. A deep voice entered her mind, her dad's. His voice reminded her of Sam Elliott. She watched movies he starred in just to hear that voice after her dad died—even the ones where he was a cowboy and there were Indians.

"If you pack your bag right, you will have everything you need. And put stuff in your pockets." As much choice as she had in what she carried, her dad had stopped her each time at the cave's opening, making her show her pockets and rummaging through her backpack. The last tugs tightening her straps.

When she opened her eyes, she found herself still clinging to the handholds, her body against the wall. She didn't want to let go of even one. But she knew she needed the items in her pocket. She steadied her feet, pushing them against the small ledges, tightened her grip in the right handhold, and slowly let go of the left, moving her hand down her body inch by inch.

The Velcro of her cargo pants released with a tear one by one of the fibers gripped together. She pulled out a crampon and a light stick, which she shook and smacked against her leg. The gesture almost unbalanced her, so she grabbed back onto the rocks. With the stick lit in neon green, she searched the wall for some softer part. One small crevice gave way to the crampon. She moved like this along the wall in painstaking and calculated movements, finding small rocks for her feet, too.

Eventually the ledge grew wide enough to come down. And again, mists of some unknown water sprayed her face in tiny droplets. A long sigh emerged from her belly, one that had waited, tight in her muscles, until she knew life still moved within her.

The darkness turned lighter. Perhaps this way led out beyond the cave. Prickles suddenly ran up and down her right arm, sharp and constant. She rubbed her arm, an attempt to settle what she thought were muscle spasms. But they weren't. She hadn't ever experienced this. It felt like what her mom called sleepy legs, but moved with a current, back and forth.

Wider and wider walkways emerged and the ceiling slowly drifted farther from her head. A large arched opening appeared, visible by some yellow light brightening. It didn't fill the room, but with such darkness, anything was enough to catch her eyes, even this small, round glow.

The air cooled. And once she passed through the arch, the ceiling reached cathedral heights, but bent and twisted into the art of the rock's own erosion. She couldn't find the light's origin. Her eyes adjusted and moved along the walls and down to the floor. Here, it rose and fell smoother than the cave's path, like someone had polished solely this part. Water had probably whorled its way through here over time, ending in this smooth pattern. She walked, her hand on the wall, her eyes roving, taking in each detail. Sometimes her fingertips and palms hit bumps or holes or cracks—imperfections that let her know she was still underground. About halfway around this room, she set her pack down and sat on the ground, legs crossed.

Her entire body filled with the cool wall and the floor. But the prickles in her arm continued, not increasing and not decreasing.

With her head against the wall, she stared at the opposite wall. There was a pattern on it, somewhat like a painting.

Up close, the paint cracked and peeled in places, or was worn away—as if other fingers had touched it like she wanted to. The colors muted like the earth they may have come from. Slowly she lifted her hand and worked the tips of her fingers, those necessary connective swirls really, across the bottom part of the painting. Nothing lifted off of the wall and the surface grooved with dips.

As she stood back to take in the figures, the images swirled along the walls. It wasn't that they moved where the people walked or the deer sprang into a sprint. They simply swirled. Her feet remained planted in place, her body unmovable. And the prickles along her right arm intensified. The movement of air became louder. It didn't howl as wind storms do. It moved along the tiny hairs in the inner ear—caresses tuning the vibrations in her head—seeming like words, but not quite. The picture blurred and became one large swirling chaos.

Her back grew warm. When she turned, a fire crackled in a small pit. *Where on earth? What is happening?* The pictographs stopped swirling—or maybe they never had. She drank more water and it hit her stomach, which, empty, felt each guzzle of the water drop into it. When she turned back to the fire, a man and woman sat, their hands held out, palms forward, warming them.

Cold had crept up her body while she explored this room. Maybe it was the loss, too, of endorphins from the climb. The cold must mean that air came from some shaft, though. Flames twisted and turned as they inched over the small logs.

The man nodded at the woman. "I think we've caught her attention."

She stepped forward, and then back again. "Where did you come from?" Peering around the room, she found no exit but the way she entered. "Did you cross the ledge, too?"

The woman giggled. Her gray hair curled at the sides of her face. Brown ringed the pupils of extraordinarily large eyes. "Honey, she doesn't know."

The man kept his eyes on her. Their black depths lit with the tips of the fire. "She'll figure it out."

"I think we should tell her."

"Come here," he said. He patted the ground next to him.

She didn't want to, but her body moved forward and she sat down. Her knees cracked as she folded her legs under her.

"The fire will warm you," said the man.

The man and woman busied themselves with shifting the logs to increase the fire. Then the woman pulled out some sort of raw meat. She tossed it onto a hot rock in the pit, but not too close to the flames.

She stared at the couple—watching them interact with eye changes and small, minute gestures someone may not notice. The woman touched his elbow and he would turn the meat. He winked and the woman turned pink. They were probably married.

The way the couple looked at each other seemed familiar—one her dad had given her mom. The long-ago image played fuzzy in her mind, though. But these two did not appear anything like them—different-colored eyes, posture, older dress. *Those clothes.*

"See, I told you," said the older man. "I can see those eyes with cogs going behind them."

She furrowed her brows. "Did you know any of my family?"

"Mmm, something like that." The light played along the ridges of the older man's face, sparking gray mustache hairs to shine silver. The thick mustache moved with his mouth and facial expressions.

She barely remembered her grandfather. In fact, most memories came from photos. The lift in this man's eyebrow seemed just like him, how he carried himself and straightened his back—though not quite a mirror image.

The man put his hand to his chin and flipped the meat. Fat dripped from the sides and hissed.

A draft wafted around the cave and passed down her body. Prickles still moved along her arm, though not as intense.

All remained silent, except for the meat turning, the stick tapping the stone, and a pot of something the man stirred. He nodded at her. She knew time wore by, but her watch was cracked, probably from her grappling with the ledge. It had stopped in that moment, and she couldn't reconfigure time in her mind.

"Is this what Dad was looking for all this time?" She motioned to the pictographs and the cave.

"No, not the cave. What it holds."

Her father had told her and her cousin stories, most of

them the traditional Creation Stories. But sometimes he spoke of family surrounding them, in the trees, in the streams, and along the roadways.

"Just listen," her dad had often said.

"So does that mean this is where you lived?" she asked the older couple.

"No," said the older man. "Not us. But relatives came here."

"Why am I meeting you, then? Why not my Dad?"

"It's not that time," the woman replied.

The man touched his wife on the shoulder.

Prickles intensified up and down her arm, and the fire died down.

"We don't always find what we seek," said the man.

She stared into the fire. Smoke filled her nostrils, along with charcoaled meat. As the smoke wafted over her, her eyes watered and she blinked several times.

When she turned toward them, the couple seemed again immersed in their own body language and eye contact. They laughed and spoke a few of the old words she didn't know, yet could sense their meaning. Joy, food, her, her father, the fire.

A connection evolved, her to them, which she could not explain. She knew them in this language of theirs. Not merely the words, but the relationship.

They finally looked at her and smiled. The older woman nodded toward her.

She nodded back.

"Which way is out?" She didn't want to go and desired to stay a while. But she had to get the guys.

The man pointed in the direction opposite to where she entered. When she turned back, they were gone. The images had not only stopped swirling, they had disappeared, and the stone fire pit had gone, leaving the cave damp again and dark. The scent of animal flesh remained in the air, letting her know she didn't need to pinch herself. A feel along the cave wall where the pictograph had been no longer revealed paint, just bumps of the cave. Yet those bumps seemed to follow the same pattern as the painting. The prickles in her arms ceased as well. She stared at the wall for a while, thinking maybe they would return. She knew, though, that those were the only moments she would have, however fleeting.

The air moved, and she followed the direction the man had pointed. The exit was a small space and eventually she had to crawl. Soon she came to a point of light where she made her way up out of the dirt and rock and grit and into more rock and scraggy grass. The climb out didn't take long, so this way in was much closer to the open space of the cave. A white pine stood in front of her, its top branches almost bare of needles. The scent lingered while she walked through trees toward the outcrop more open and holding less vegetation. The walk grew steadily steeper. A half hour later, the cave opening stood up the hill from her—the boys just emerging from its mouth surrounded by rounded boulders. Her cousin saw her.

"How'd you get out here first?" he asked.

"I came out a different end." She pointed.

His eyes narrowed, but he shrugged.

"So," the boy with glasses said, "what did you see on your end?"

She knew he meant rocks or weird creatures. That one loved to find all the creepy things.

Her cousin tugged on her pack. "Let's go guys, get it together to leave. You can swap stories on the way down."

She put her hand on his arm. "I don't think we should go

yet." Her voice was soft. She tried to pull her cousin back. The hours during the funeral returned to her. She remembered her cousin in a corner, silent tears streaming down his face and dripping onto his shirt. Her shadow in the doorway made him look up. His eyes had turned black. He turned, staring out the window, unmoving. She put her hand out to touch his shoulder, and he flinched. So she had left him there by that window.

He pushed her off. "We're later than planned. It'll get dark."

"I saw them."

"Saw who?"

"Our ancestors."

He stopped, all body movement frozen except his breath, with chest raising and lowering, raising and lowering. "That's not possible."

"Of course—"

"No. Now we found his cave. That's going to have to be *enough* of him."

"I wasn't looking for him."

"Weren't you?"

"What was it *you* were looking for?" she asked.

Red crawled up his neck in several blotches. His mouth clenched shut, then opened. "Listen here, boys. This one says she found her ancestors in that cave."

The other three suddenly became quiet.

"Isn't that funny. Ghosts in all that wet and rock."

"We see them," she said. "You know we do. They're here for us." She reached out to touch his arm, and for a few seconds, he let her hold her hand there.

"You think just because we have brown skin—we can see that stuff?" Her cousin swung his eyes to the corner of the lids and made a *phhuh* noise. "Oh, but wait, maybe the milky white skin can."

The boys laughed and hiccupped—more out of nervous habit. They turned to go, leaning over laughing hard. Their backs grew smaller as they started on the trail back down the hills.

She walked down the hill. She knew what she saw. Her cousin's hair swayed along his back, brown and longer than hers. She turned around, noticing the outline to the cave changing, darkening in the falling light. Soon, it would be engulfed in the black.

Even when she was young, she recognized these differences between her and her cousins. Her tribal relations made connections harder when the line evolved from the paternal side and she lost status. A chasm seemed to exist within that and her off-rez upbringing.

Perhaps her dad always walked so deeply into the caverns—carrying out rocks, quartz, and mica—to tie him to these moments.

"It's pushing through. It will reach you. Don't forget." Her father stroked her hair. At seven, her head met his chest.

"What does, Daddy?"

"Your blood. It is Haudenosaunee."

"Why don't we live on the reservation, then?"

He shrugged. "Not quite right, I guess. Your grandfather thought this was better."

"Is it?"

"Better? I don't know. It's what we know, though."

Nya:weh Dad.

His voice echoed in her head. It floated in the trees. It moved over the line of boys dropping down rocky embankment. And it reverberated behind her in the caves, hanging from the stalactites, and crowding the dark spaces.

The Crack in the Bridge

I peer down past the stone wall. Those damn muskrats are there again. Circling in the Genesee River for no reason. This wasn't exactly cattail land, though. But they've been there my whole life, pretty far back. I shake my head. *Avoid.*

The Lower Falls stand to my right, splashing down, making rapids out of the water below. Some white person's legend says that there's a white doe, a woman who jumps over the edge with her man and turns into a deer. Who does that? Certainly not a Seneca woman. Apparently when you see the white doe, that's her protecting you or the land or some craziness like that. I've never seen one. But my uncle's got bunches he photographed and framed. Some obsession.

The muskrats chirp when they surface. *So annoying.* I cross the other side. The bridge makes getting to the other canyon part easier. I wondered how anyone did that before the man-made connection.

Some of the steps look slick with mud from constant

dripping water and runoff. You can tell the water comes often because some stone steps are now just mud, degraded so far you wonder if they will wash away with a heavy rain.

There's not much to this side. I can walk to Mt. Morris from here. Why I even cross over, I don't know. When I climb the boulders near the steps, I can see far below where rocks and water meet and crash against one another. There is a large-trunked tree growing up and over the boulder. Higher than most trees. The sign says to stay off. But this view is always worth disobeying. I can't feel the falls misting. But it wouldn't rid the September-extended summer humidity anyway. I wipe my neck and try to get rid of the ugly sweat forming.

And they're calling to me. I've learned their language over the years. So I kind of know what they say, but I can't put it into English. They're not speaking Seneca, either. I've had these moments growing up where I'd watch YouTube videos over and over, them calling, making striking noises when they dive, me deciphering what it all meant.

Mom tells me from when I am little and on up to listen to dreams. I so often wondered if I dream when I see the musk-rats. Like daydreaming. I do that a lot. Some teacher could be talking, or my new boss, and off my mind goes imagining a different life or the upcoming evening I might spend with friends. Only I see these muskrats. That can happen with things we're led to know. But why they show up when I don't want them to, I don't know.

I hear my name. My sister is here. No surprise. She knows I'm visiting Mom, which means I'll come here. They both do that. They check in on me when I go here like I'm still five. But good Lord, I'm twenty-seven.

My sister can track me like no other person. It's probably because when I am three, we visit here, and I climb over on the stone bridge when no one is looking. I even dangle off the side. I'm so drawn to that refreshing water. And that's the first muskrat call.

Leave it to the ancestors to give me something weird.

I never fall that day. My sister grabs my hand and somehow pulls me up. That's some strong eight-year-old move.

We never visit this area, so I don't come back until I have my license and explore one day. I had forgotten about those muskrats. Now, here I am whenever I visit from Rochester.

I sigh. "Over here."

"Get down from those rocks. Are you kidding me?"

Good Lord. Big sister. More like mother.

How do I even explain our dinners? Mom cooks, but really shouldn't. Her bread is all soggy that night. And the sauce tastes so fishy. Like sea salt and salmon got all up in there. I try not to make faces. She doesn't even eat fish.

But mostly, Mom and Sis talk. The entire time. They just go on about their own jobs and lives and kind of talk over me. They volley back and forth; it's so boring. Who only talks about work? Dad simply sits back, eating. He rarely says more than two words. He's retired from the salt mines. Happened right after one of his friends died of a heart attack.

"How's your job?" Mom stops midbite, her fork rolled with spaghetti.

"Oh," I say. "It's good. Just fixing some outdated webpages. Designing the fonts and backgrounds and what things will look like."

"That's nice, honey. You get that promotion yet?" she asks.

My sister nods along like she's listening to me.

"It's more like a raise right now. Those get reviewed this fall."

Mom makes a noise that's her agreeing. "I hear your sister found you by that bridge again. I want you staying away from there."

My sister gives me this hard look, close to *I told you so*. She doesn't want anything causing Mom worry. Although Mom worries too much anyway. So how we're the cause, I'm not sure.

When I'm drying the dishes, Sis pulls me around. She even pinches the skin around my upper arm. "Ow. Seriously?"

"You need to listen. Stay away from there. You can't be going overboard. You're creating too much ruckus always going there and making Mom feel bad."

"She doesn't feel bad."

"I told you, no more." Her eyes are this deep black. She gets like that. So angry with the world but taking it out on us. "You just drop all this."

Geez. She is so deep sometimes. I live too far away. I never talk to Mom. I need to learn to take care of myself. That's your run-of-the-mill Sis talk.

I live an hour away and talk to Mom more than she does. I also invite Mom places for more than some half-hour quickie dinner. And I have a good job, my own car, and a credit card I always pay off. But the younger sister never gets respect.

Sis'll never notice those things. As far as that worry, well, maybe I am responsible, maybe I'm not. I do go to those muskrats most every time. Sometimes, they call me in my dreams. Not the waking ones when I'm there. But I never tell anyone that. I also don't tell Sis when I go to the park. I don't go every time. I keep it quiet when I do. I can't tell my family anything.

The drive back to Rochester isn't long, but the next morning, I need two lattes. Families are exhausting. So are those dreams. Had one again last night. The muskrat makes this sound, a high one, and slinks along the water with ebbs and flows.

Those dreams are fitful. I still hear mom telling us about our dreams. The images mean something. I used to think she makes things up, especially when my teachers have patted my arm, shaken their heads, and explained how magic doesn't really exist.

I think maybe I ought to take a sleeping pill. Sis uses them every night "to shut out the extras." She gives me a few to try a month ago when I complain about our genetic dark under-eye circles.

With water and a chug around ten the next night, I feel drowsy. Once my head hits the firm pillow, I'm out.

The next morning, I don't remember anything. No dreams. Not even brushing my teeth. My body moves slowly, though, almost heavy. More coffee is necessary.

Gus's Subs has this great homemade bread, softer and thicker than Subway's, and real meat, not the deli kind stuffed with preservatives. A line forms around the corner. Sis texts several times asking about Mom's birthday. What should we get her? Could we do something together? And what about next year's big sixtieth? A year ahead. *Good Lord.*

Once inside, halfway through the line, my head becomes cloudy, woozy. Those are some of the pill's side effects. Man. I close my eyes, then open them. My arms are heavy, and I feel like I'm walking through Jell-O rather than air.

A woman behind me taps my shoulder. "Hey, you can move up now."

My vision blurs. I order the usual. Susan, the cashier, recognizes me. Even Susan's voice sounds strange. I think Susan says, "We're swimming."

"What?" I ask.

"I didn't say anything. Just waiting for you to pay." Susan's voice stays chipper.

"Oh." I hand her cash and put the leftover change in the tip jar.

The paper bag they hand me is oily. Dripping in oil. Grease spots have formed and penetrate the paper. I certainly didn't ask for an oil dressing today.

A large park is nearby. Easy to get to and back in time and still have most of the hour with nothing but me and the people who pass by. I eat the pickle spear first. Brine hits my tongue, and, man, my brain tingles again, the numbness dissipating.

Apple next. I really want salty tastes along my tongue, so I leave the meat until last. Unwrapping the sandwich, I see no oil. In fact, nothing escapes the bread, not even the mayo or tomatoes.

I must be tired. Just not myself.

The rest of the day goes as usual, questions from coworkers and problem-solving a downed website. Once home, though, I sit down on my couch and fall asleep.

Suddenly, I'm underwater. Swimming in my living room, breathing in the water. The water feels warm, but the sensation of being wet doesn't exist. *What are those muskrats doing now?* I float over my couch, hit my head on the patio sliding doors, and make my way to the kitchen.

Gray. Everything's gray and murky. No light penetrates the

water, but yet I can see everything, not just as shapes, but as their actual selves.

My body suddenly falls flat to the kitchen tiles and stays on those cold squares.

That next morning I somehow drive to work.

My boss catches me listening to those muskrats again. I thought she would say "get back to work." But instead, she launches into this family story.

"We were in San Diego last summer, up in the La Jolla Cove area. There's this beach where the sea lions hang out. It's all fenced because it's one of their main parks. But boy, that smell. Still, they seemed to . . ." She doesn't finish. Her eyes wander and stare out my one office window. The building stretches high, and you can see this bank out there with a top that almost looks like a hand reaching up.

"Karen?"

"Hmm. Oh yeah. Well, it was just beautiful. The water washing over the rocks. Them calling and barking. Moms up against their pups. But pinch your nose." She laughs. "Not the same as those things." She points at my screen. "Is it? Those are rather creepy. All slinking about."

I explain that's their hunting sounds and movements. They're looking for something.

She walks out. But not before shaking her finger. *Get back to work.*

I keep their sounds on with headphones while I crank work out.

That must have affected the dreams again. I'm underwater, this time with a green-and-brown coloring that washes away all other color. Seems like some lens cover, but I can't wipe it away. And I can't hear anything.

Tossing and turning, I finally wake up. My hair's wet. I wrap the strands up and try sleeping again. But don't. I really am kind of scared in that water. My heart just pumps as if I'm really there. And those muskrat eyes, small round eyes, they look so human if you stare straight in though.

The next night, I sit up and struggle to breath, gulping air and grabbing my throat. Hair, clothes, the bedding, everything is dry. I can only see the green digits on the nightstand clock. I breathe deeper each time, then slow.

Wow, that's a vivid dream. I run my hand through my hair, and there's something. A piece of a long, wet leaf, half-rotted.

My brain. I can't feel it. I've been disconnected for weeks, thinking I'm one place, but sometimes being elsewhere.

The muskrats. They keep at it. Keep appearing daylight or nighttime.

They don't go away, no matter what. If I take the sleeping pills, now they have the gall to come when I'm awake.

Dark circles take over my eyes.

I finally drive back home.

"Are you doing okay?" my mother asks me.

Sis isn't there. I haven't seen Mom in a month and know if I don't have dinner with her, she'll drive to my workplace and ask my coworkers about me. "It's for your own good," she says when I'm younger. She even once walks right into my history class demanding to see the history text. The teacher's face loses all color, then red slowly creeps up his neck and into his ears. From then on, my mother tells us stories and sends us to visit two elders, one every other weekend.

I can't help but roll my eyes when Mom checks in. "I'm fine, Mom."

"You look awful. They treating you right at that job?"

"My job is great. Don't you dare go see my boss." She piles more food onto my plate.

"Good. You're eating more."

The muskrats have stayed away and faded the closer I get home.

Mom spoons more canned green beans onto my plate.

I hate these green beans. Such a bitter taste. Didn't know I even liked green beans until a lunch at my friend Beth's house where they steamed green beans right out of their garden. Damn can.

Chewing tiny bites doesn't make the flavor change. Then they start to taste fishy. I cough and drink half a glass of milk.

I think about that water, right over the hills in the park. A space taken by William Pryor Letchworth. Mary Jemison forced to sell her land. Seneca land. I sigh.

"Mom, you know those stories Grandpa told, the ones about muskrat and raven?"

"Yes. He really taught some lessons to you kids."

"Have you seen muskrats around here?"

I notice Dad stops eating. He says nothing, though.

Mom laughs direct from the belly, and she yelps in the middle, like a hiccup and a laugh.

"I take it no."

"Well, I also haven't been out and about in the woods in a long while." Mom pauses, her fork halfway to her mouth. "We do have important relations with the muskrat. Why?"

"Nothing." My head pounds.

"When you were a girl, you had some strange dreams about our stories. Got those dark circles just like you have there, too."

Even though my mom continues eating, she furrows her brows and clucks. "Pay attention to their details. The dreams went away whenever you did."

"But what does seeing details do?"

"You never explained once you got to see them."

Thub thub. Thub thub. My head keeps running.

Lunch gets quiet, and we talk mostly about the flowers in Mom's yard she just cut back before frosts. She hates the grocery flowers but puts some in vases, and the roses have opened in that way where they appear huge and curled. The yellow ones with pink centers are my favorite.

I don't always know where conversation should go between us. Maybe neither one of us has that kind of life where talk happens. I work. I go home. I hang with friends. No boyfriend. She works. Has the house, my sister, silent Pop, and goes to the library or grocery store. There was so much more when I was in high school. But maybe it was just more going on, but not substance. Does that seem like family?

My dad pulls me aside before I leave. "Everything all right?"

I stare, then say, "Sure, Dad."

He puts a hand on my arm. "I don't believe you."

His look is deep. I haven't seen this reaction before. "Dad?"

"They'll ask you to do something important. They've been at you long enough." He nods.

I stare after his back, confused.

I hug Mom. We usually just wave goodbye. But she squeezes extra hard.

The dreams become these intense images. Sometimes there's only water and rocks. Sometimes there's muskrats swimming around me. I feel blasts of wet and wind and cold. Piled blankets are not enough to stave away the chill, even though my windows are closed.

I wake so often with sweats, brain fog, and loss of breath.

People look at me sideways now when I walk by. Whispers. Maybe the greasy hair that never goes away scares them. Or the large under-eye bags. Or the clothes that somehow don't fit anymore. Everything about me has shrunk.

I don't dare visit Mom. She'd think I'm in some kind of trouble. I call, so she doesn't worry. I just fake busy.

I keep listening to muskrat calls online. There's something to them. Inherently, words translate in my mind, but not English. I think I understand what they're saying now.

Calling and calling.

Underwater songs travel faster. Not like the chirping of land calls. No longer weird or Pink Floyd–like to my ears, I play them over and over and over. I don't think anyone else hears. But I imagine this is how they navigate the water.

If anyone enters my office, I make them shove off. People scurry away. When my boss makes comments, the words float and float.

I stop going to work after that. I can't focus. Maybe they ask me to leave. It doesn't matter. Now I get to listen.

Calling continues. I don't think I should drive. Drive there where they are. Where they wait. Fall turns into winter. Almost. The cold invigorates my skin, though. Brings a glisten to the layers of wet. I like it.

My hands feel strange wrapped around some wheel, feet working pedals. All weird. All out of sorts. The whole way.

But what is in sorts?

That isn't me.

But then my feet crumble leaves and crack tiny twigs.

Down the stone steps. Past the stone walls.

Some black squirrel chitters after me.

The water crashes loud as always.

I recognize their language, and I know what they're saying. It's old, old Seneca. But I can't hear that right now. I just can't. My heart is agoing with some heavy *thump-thump*.

Except for this spot, I've always seemed to know this area, like a string that ties you, but you can't explain. Let's be clear, I'm no nature lover. No matter these muskrats and this place. That's not the tie here. It's everything. Everything in its place. Which is why that moment, I understand. I understand the years spent called, seeing these creatures that aren't really there.

On the bridge.

The muskrats circle below. Their tails sometimes overlapped. Back and forth. My head spins, blurring the edges of my vision. Blurring until I see nothing. Until I hear the underwater calls.

Standing on top of the bridge wall, I see so far below, further than the rocks. Maybe even straight through an endless bottom.

Then I'm there.

They swim around me. I can breathe again. Feel the air flowing through my skin, up under some layers, warming me.

I move, slither, racing through the water, no longer too shallow for us. No longer rocks and rapids and waterfalls or frozen, full of ice. I call and call. And the others swim around me, paws touching here and there.

My body floats and glides. We force water away and around us, sail over rocks we shouldn't be able to sail over, wiggle down rapids, and move so far from that bridge. I no longer see the stones, the gray, the falls. Or hear my mom's voice. I see the muskrats and even more animals. All around me, guiding me through cold waters. Sonar radiating along the waves. I forget the other world. I am called and there below me, I see through to the other side of the world, so deep, so dark, so light.

And then I fall.

Luck Stone

The sun had come out, breaking through large, round clouds, which had taken over the city that week. Sometimes gray days clung on like that here. The leaves would change soon. Cam held her bike helmet under her arm and a few books in the opposite hand. She shifted her weight, having stood in line for ten minutes already.

The poor woman seemed stuck checking out all the patrons that morning. She had seen this librarian before, usually shelving, though. Her deft with the check-out machines appeared slow, although methodical. She swiped one book at a time, then put the book in a pile, straightening each book each time.

People were gasping, shaking their heads, and rocking back and forth, an impatience hard to ignore.

"Where's that young girl?" one woman said behind her. "She always goes so fast. Just click, click, click."

Cam remembered standing in lines any time she checked out books. But then, she generally came at this time, right before her classes. Seemed popular.

When she placed her books down, the woman did just as she had while they all waited.

"How are you?" she asked. Her nameplate said "Nancy." Her hair sprung up with multiple medium curls, making it seem short.

"Good. A bit gloomy outside."

"Oh, don't I know it. Seems to have kept some staff home with colds. Those poor kids."

Cam smiled. "Does make you want to curl up. But the sun came out." She pushed her hair behind her ear.

"Oh good. That's good." As they talked, the woman actually sped up. She found a rhythm. "This is a great book." Nancy held up *The Round House* by Louise Erdrich. "Won that award. But most people, they don't like that ending."

"A friend told me it was life altering."

"I agree. Stories are that way, aren't they? Those end twists." She giggled and handed Cam a due-date slip.

As she turned to leave, Nancy touched her arm. "Wait. Take this."

"What is it?" Cam held an oblong, flat rock. Smooth black-ish-green something. She didn't know.

"A luck stone." Nancy's smile beamed, and she waved the person behind her forward.

"Oh." Cam had trouble moving. She stepped aside, but stood there peering at the stone. She turned it over, then over again. The stone really was smooth, as if someone else had done this repetitively.

Luck stone? She shrugged. Whatever. The woman was clearly odd. Nice, but odd. Cam put the stone in her jeans' pocket.

She biked along the busy sidewalk toward Rochester Institute of Technology. Probably she should be biking on the streets, but she got nervous so close to cars. Who knew if they paid any attention to her small ten-speed. As each pedal moved, she felt the stone. A round, thin impediment marking her thigh.

If she stopped at the library, she was usually late to class. But as she rode, she encountered no stops, no people to curve around. The breeze blew and cooled her forehead. When she dismounted, she still felt clean, rather than sweaty. *Nice.* She clicked the helmet button and ran in, backpack on and helmet under her arm.

Used to closing the door quietly, she did so, only to see a mostly empty room. This time, she sat up front and opened her book while others arrived. American History to 1700. She preferred current topics. But her adviser suggested it for her cultural anthropology major. She wanted to focus on Rochester and stay in the area. Maybe law or politics.

Pop quiz. Easy questions. Unusual.

Some guy even stopped her after class, asking directions to the gym. He blushed and kept staring at her. "You're cute," he said. He wrote his phone number on her hand.

She stared at the digits long after he left. She hadn't had a real date. Ever. Just some agreed-upon boyfriend/girlfriend labels in middle school. She didn't wash her hand until copying the numbers.

A scratch-off lottery ticket. Ten dollars.

B+ paper in Social Justice.

Class canceled for Anthropology 200.

Clear traffic back home.

The stone was warm in her palm. She turned it over again. The shine mesmerized her. *Hmm. Does this actually work?*

"Hey, Cam. You ready for dinner?" her dad called.

"Oh. Yeah. What are we having?" She zipped the stone into her backpack. The kitchen shone with afternoon light. September brought out the sun at times, which surprised her.

"Weather changes these days," her dad said.

"Dad!"

"Global warming is real. Our ancestors knew this was bad for us."

She rolled her eyes when he talked about relatives she didn't know. And he hadn't even met. Super weird.

The hot pan sizzled. Oil and pasta mixed with veggies and peanut sauce. Heat filled the room, and she breathed in garlic and ginger.

"Yum, Dad."

"My daughter deserves stir fry today." He kissed her forehead.

"Why today?"

"I don't know. I felt *compelled*. Got out early today, too. The boss was feeling good about our sales."

Cam kissed his cheek. She wished her dad had gone to college. But she had come along. He swore he preferred her over books. Still, she hated seeing him work people to sell a car. The back of his head had a large bald spot and gray hairs poked out, years of just them marked right there.

"You going to hit the books tonight?"

"I didn't get any homework today."

"What?"

"I know! Do you want to play a round of rummy?"

The next days were much the same. Things went smoothly. Cam had known good days, but not perfect ones. That's what they felt like. Perfect. The stone warmed in her hand throughout the day. At first, the stone gave her a vibe she didn't like. It made her leave the rock at home. Like a push-pull though, she was drawn back.

Cam experimented during the following weeks. A few times the stone was in the pocket of her thrown-off jeans. Somehow, on certain days the stone appeared in her pockets without her knowing. It seemed that as long as she carried the stone, though, in her pocket or bag or purse, Cam experienced days better than even the one before. Twenties appeared on the ground. Lights turned green. Homework was light. Grades were high.

"Dad?" After a month, she wanted answers. He always knew odd details about life. "Dad?" She plunked her keys on their coffee table. That and googling hadn't answered anything else.

A note on the counter read, *Had to fill in at work. I'll be back late. See you in the morning.*

Fall meant extra hours. She sighed. The stone wasn't with her. That explained his absence.

Cam called him. She tapped the pen by the note. It rang several times before she ran up to her room and grabbed the stone.

"Cam?"

"Dad!"

"Everything okay, hon?"

"Sure. I wanted to talk. Do you have a break?" She rolled the stone through her fingers.

"Just on it."

"Dad, are there things, you know, objects that hold powers? Does that work ever?"

"Well that's direct and strange. What's going on?"

"It was something brought up in class."

"Hmm. Okay. Well, yes, sometimes objects hold power. Remember our false face masks?"

"Yeah."

"Depends on who made it or the history behind it."

"History?"

"Yeah. Things can hold energies. That's all. You can smudge and bring in positive energies to balance things."

"Okay, but what if it's positive itself? Giving?"

"I don't know. I've never heard of objects giving things. You sure everything is okay?"

"Of course, Dad."

"I have to go. See you at home."

The stone fit Cam's hand, perfectly. What was the harm in good days?

Cam continued her easy semester, enjoying finally being a straight-A student.

"Wow, Cam. You're so lucky!" said Sarah. She sat in Cam's oversized lounge chair. They knew each other from high school, and now had two classes together. But they had never been close. She liked this girl's constant talk about movies and her curiosity about phenomena like conspiracy theories. "Did you know about the signs on the dollar bill? The eye in the pyramid? It was on the Great Seal, first. Then Roosevelt put it on the dollar. They say Illuminati. I say, government eyes."

Cam nodded. She wanted to laugh, but held it in. She really did like hearing her talk. And some of those theories might be true. Who knows.

"There's like some kind of bubble around you lately. Protective." Sarah bit into a large pizza slice. She yelped. "Dammit. Hot!" She tended to jump around like that.

Cam picked off the peppers and took a few bites. The sauce was sweet with a slight kick. She licked her fingers when she finished. Cam still wasn't totally sure her luck lately was fully the stone. Something told her never to leave the house without it, though. Inside the house, she forgot about the smooth texture and colors that melted together. Colors that when she carried the stone, she pulled out just to stare at.

Sarah saw her the day before with the stone in her palm, staring. Cam shrugged off the questions. But Sarah was clearly drawn too. She had even reached out her hand until Cam hurried the stone into her bag.

"Hey, let me see that stone. Where did you put it?" Sarah's eyes grew large. "Come on. It's so cool."

Cam wondered if Sarah knew. But she didn't, right? Cam had thought about asking the librarian what was going on. But she couldn't bring herself to go back to that library. It was strange. Cam loved books. And she couldn't let go of that stone. At all. She didn't know what would happen if she saw the woman. She no longer felt strange vibes about the rock, though. Just vibes that . . . fit.

"My dad's got it."

But Cam caught Sarah rolling the stone in her hand when she came back with drinks.

"Sarah, you should put that down."

"Oh come on. You've had this thing all these weeks, hogging it." She put the stone in her hoodie pocket.

"Give it back!" Cam grabbed Sarah's shirt and pulled the stone out. Power surged through her, rolling within her blood, quick and heavy, like she hadn't known. A harsh strength.

"Hey." Sarah jumped Cam, but Cam kept her hands under her, one over the other, the stone protected. She squeezed her eyelids tight together. Sarah pulled her hair. *Ow! What the hell? It's a stone.*

She wished Sarah would stop. *Right now!*

The pounding suddenly ended. And Sarah was gone.

Had she walked out? Cam looked around. She held the stone out and away from her.

Where is Sarah? Her heart tumbled against her chest.

"Dad? Dad?" Cam yelled until hoarse, but he wasn't home, yet.

She put the stone in her bag and backed away. Then pulled the stone out again, the colors mesmerizing her. Cam closed her eyes. *Come on, Cam.* But the stone went back in her pocket. Flat. Her breath moved faster and faster. She remained in her room, seated, holding her knees, back against the wall. The floorboards were cold.

When the lock snapped back and the front door shut an hour later, her breathing slowed.

"Dad?"

"Hey, honey."

"What do you know about stones?"

"Good evening to you too, Cam." His cheeks twitched and eyebrow raised.

She took a deep breath. "Can they hold powers?"

"My mom said they could. Some are healing. Some a bit cranky. Why?" He drew out the last syllable.

"Nothing." The rock heated her pocket.

"Is this about that call last week?"

"No. Just, something someone said."

"You want dinner?" He boiled water in a large pot and threw pasta in. But he kept staring at her, his eyes still dark.

She watched him stir, forever standing by that window. That's how she knew him. When her mom died, Cam was too young to know her at just three. Pictures were the only source of knowledge about her mom. Her dad didn't say much. But then again, Cam didn't ask. Her questions always made her dad sad.

Her dad had pictures of her mother scattered across the house. Some only her, some her and him, some all three of them. There was one in her own bedroom, with Cam and her mother when she was maybe a year old. Her mother looked down at her, her mouth open as if she was talking, midconversation. Cam, though, faced the camera.

Just last week, there he was, staring at a picture, holding one from his nightstand. He had left his door open and she caught this as she passed by.

No matter what she tried, she simply could not remember her mother. No smell, no sound, no images. This bothered her. But her sadness didn't match her dad's.

Last year, she wanted her dad to try online dating. He simply shook his head no and that was the end of it.

"Come on," he said. He warmed pasta sauce from a jar, with no time to make his homemade marinara.

They sat down, the sun setting. The changing light turned their garden yellow. Her dad had been cultivating the small yard, turning the land so many colors with vegetables and flowers since her mother died.

The steam drifted and her face warmed. "It's getting to be fall finally. That warm up held it off." She even tasted fall in the pasta sauce. Cam was sure her dad had added a little cayenne pepper and cinnamon.

"How's school?" he asked.

"Same. Good grades."

"That's my girl."

She couldn't smile back. She wasn't sure she was really earning her grades. They came to her more like winning numbers on a lottery ticket. Flutters looped around in her stomach. She put her fork down.

"You good, Cam?"

"Of course. I ate too much with Sarah."

"Where is Sarah? Will she ever stay for dinner?"

"Uhh, home." Cam rinsed her plate, red sauce spreading and spreading into the sink.

"You two are getting close this year. That's nice. You need some girlfriends."

"Yeah." She had trouble breathing again. Cam couldn't believe Sarah had just . . . vanished. She slowed her breathing. People don't just disappear. "We kind of had a fight."

"Oh?" He said no more. He often waited like that with her.

Her dad reached out and hugged her. He squeezed and let go. "What if we go fishing tomorrow morning?"

"That'd be great Dad."

"Guess we had better hit the sack." He laughed.

She awoke early. Earlier than even necessary for fishing. She groaned. *Don't get up. Don't get up. Not now*. She rolled over, but the hallway light her dad left on trickled under the door.

Okay. She threw her legs over her bed. The clock said 3:30. She would have to get up in a half hour anyway. Her eyes nearly shut, she opened her closet door. Light circled her coat pocket.

The luck stone.

She couldn't handle anymore lost people. She slammed the door and leaned against the wood. *Seriously. Seriously*.

Cam swore she heard the swirling light make a sound. One she couldn't place.

It was just a stone. Right? Sarah left . . . embarrassed.

Deep down, Cam knew differently.

She opened the door. The light was still glowing in the

162

pocket. She pulled out the stone. Light shone through it, illuminating a butterfly shape. She had always thought something was there among the dark patterns.

She had had the luck stone for over a month now. She felt good with it around, but at the same time, she could only explain the feeling as out-of-body. Not herself. Good things happened, but she didn't *feel* better.

A voice she couldn't place, but knew was unconnected to the stone, said, "Fix it."

Bring Sarah back.

Sarah appeared, curled on the floor, midpounding. She looked at her hands, then at Cam. "Oh." She slowly rose. "I've got to get home."

Cam opened her bedroom door.

"Sorry." Sarah's eyes became dark.

"Me too."

The stone's light faded.

Cam found a loose board in the closet and tossed the stone in the gap. Her breath let out long and slow.

The water held a glisten only the early morning could create. Quiet moved all around the two figures, her and her dad. She tried being quiet, had often warned her dad about how much this being still wouldn't work for her. He knew talking was her way, but ignored her trait here.

"If the fish will bite, they will bite," he had told her.

She went fishing whenever he asked. They rented a boat from a friend along with his truck a few days a year.

The breeze covered her body, sending fall chills her way. The river swayed their boat. Not a short ride, the St. Lawrence

River was his favorite spot, but he could rarely go there. So this was his go-to, Lake Ontario. Her fishing pole hit the boat, clanging against the floor.

"Crap. Oh, sorry, Dad."

"No worries." He handed her the pole. "You get some sleep last night?"

"Yeah. Just up earlier thinking."

"Okay." He reeled his line in, ever so gently. The bobber made its way to their boat once surfaced. Then he cast again. His arch, perfect, both with arm and line. "These fish can take talk, Cam. No need to worry."

She attempted a smile, which formed contorted. She cast her line, and the hook stuck somewhere in the boat. Two minutes later she found where, while her father chuckled.

Once her recast hit the water, although roughly, she shifted. "Dad, what was Mom like?" She swallowed. Her heart beat so fast, she had to take deep breaths.

He wound his reel, pulling the line in, nothing hooked.

When she turned, he was watching out the other end of the boat. He cast again, sat back, the seat enveloping him. "She was special." The words were almost soundless, almost lost. "We had such few years together. But her beauty and the way she stood for things. Cared deeply . . . She worked at a daycare on the rez. That was her. In a nutshell."

The two didn't speak again. But in the car ride back when their song came on, the one they always sang along to, the music turned up loud, their voices carried the tune together.

Her bedroom was quite warm, more than usual. But her dad hadn't turned the heat up. At least not at night during fall. She held the picture, just her and her mom, and peered toward her dad's room. The door was shut tonight. Sometimes when he was very tired he did that.

She had a thought. *What if* . . . Power filled her hands. Her head. Her blood going again.

Cam was overcome. She knew she could do anything. Create anything. That was what this was—she was creating. Like her dad casting a line, rippling the water.

With that realization, a small light appeared surrounding her, warm and soft. The butterfly shape appeared and then faded. The stone's light left.

Cam stood there a moment. She closed her eyes and mentally sensed her body, searching for signs of luck. She didn't feel lucky. But then again, she never had *felt* it. Whatever *it* was. She couldn't tell.

Her room was normal. Bed. Shelves. Closet. Window. Check. Still mint green with the stitched quilt full of flowers by her mom. *Shit.* Nothing changed. *Shit shit.* Something clanged downstairs.

Dad. One of his late-nights snacks. She ran downstairs, her feet clomping, echoing on the wood. Maybe it was toasted cheese.

Light hit her eyes and momentarily blocked her kitchen view. Then, there she was. Her mother. Stirring some sauce, the window framing the darkened night behind her. Her long hair flowed down her back, black and straight.

"Oh."

"There you are, honey. I was heating myself up a snack." Her mother looked at Cam as if they had spoken that morning. *Snack? Pasta sauce? Wasn't it late?* A large smile, her skirt crumpled, but fitted to her body perfectly. There were gray strands sprinkled in her hair and small wrinkles along the eyes. She was pretty. Different from the photos, though. Aged maybe.

"Mom?"

"Yeah. Of course."

"But—"

"Come here." Her mother reached out and hugged Cam. She squeezed hard. "There. Go grab some plates."

Cam looked around. Decorations were the same. Colors. Backyard. Even the plates she pulled out of the hutch—cream with purple loops.

"This looks good to go," her mother said. She spooned pasta and sauce on the plates and then served a side salad with radishes and carrots.

She hated radishes. Some snack.

"Mom?"

"You keep doing that." Her laugh was loud and it pierced Cam's ears.

"Mom. Where's Dad?"

Her mother sat down and put her hands together. "I didn't know if you would know."

"Know what?"

"He would have wanted this."

"What's going on, Mom?"

"You know, sweetie. You did it."

"What do you mean? Where's Dad?"

"Honey, he . . ." She paused and looked down. "It's just me and you, babe."

Cam choked and spit out her pasta. "I never—!"

"I know. But, that's how it worked." Her mother shrugged. "It will be okay." She patted Cam's arm.

Cam felt a chill. Her body shivered, fully shaking out of her control.

They ate. The pasta needed salt. Her mother talked as if she had been there Cam's whole life—without her dad. She knew that Cam had scraped her knee climbing the backyard tree, her major, the classes she took, which ones she got As in.

"And what about that young man? The one who helped you the other day. He was cute. Gave you his number, right?"

Cam raised her eyebrow. Her heart was beating so fast she almost couldn't catch her breath. Dad wouldn't have asked. She and her dad, they were just . . . in sync. Knew things without ever asking.

The water ran over Cam's hands, suds forming as she scraped off sauce. Then she used her fingers to scrub the oil from the salad bowls. Cam let the water run hot, turning her hands red, almost burning them.

"What do you want to do now, honey? Watch a movie? Rom-com okay?"

"Yeah. Sure." *Did she ever sleep?*

She sat down. Her mother's body radiated warmth. The movie was funny. But Cam couldn't get her mind off the changes. Well, the one change. Though there seemed to be different DVDs in their zippered case. Too many romances throughout the various sleeves. And how was her mom happy? Okay.

When credits rolled, Cam said, "So Dad knows this is what happened?"

"I think so, baby."

"Why wouldn't he fight to come back? You know, come through with you?"

"I don't think he could any more than I could have."

Her mother put the DVD back in its case. She fiddled with the zipper. "I'm going to heat up some hot cider. You in?"

Cam nodded. But she swallowed and felt bile move up her trachea.

The microwave beeped. Clanging ceramic and glass followed.

"Here." Her mother handed her a mug.

The heat spread through her fingers and palms. Her face got warm, too. Cam blew, lifting the spoon and trying to cool the liquid she knew would burn.

"Shopping tomorrow?" her mother asked.

"I'm not much of a shopper."

"Come on. We'll get you some new clothes. Some things to go with your school year." She rubbed Cam's knee.

Cam had to hold her knee in place so it wouldn't jump. "I miss him." *This is all wrong.*

"I know. I can't replace him. But now I get to be here." She motioned for Cam to move closer.

Cam paused. She slid over, and they were elbow to elbow. Her mother's appeared white and ashy. Her father's skin was more olive, but her mother's was the milky version of his, which made the ashiness harder to see. He was Seneca, her mother Mohawk. Two nations and two people connected long ago. But Cam couldn't imagine that connection right then.

She touched her mother's hand.

"See, it's all right," said her mother. She reached around Cam.

The two hugged.

"I love you, Mom. But I'm sorry."

The luck stone warmed Cam's pocket. The heat bit her side, and she knew there would be a mark left behind.

Phillip

On Sundays, Phillip would walk into church, scuffed knees, his shirt backwards or untucked at times, and smelling like the fields. I don't know if it was due to slowness or shyness or sheer dumb luck. But Phillip was just full of ignorance. He would walk right up to the front pews and plop himself before the pulpit. The look in his eyes always moved into pure awe when the preacher spoke. You never saw Phillip fall asleep or lose interest. But those around him sat further away, noticing only the smell and the loud sounds emerging during hymns that one could only assume were notes somewhere on the scales of Heaven. Phillip never noticed the stares or nose pinching, and he never changed his seat.

I had known him since he was a child, nearly twenty years ago. He lived in a small, square hut made out of boards and old shingles at the edge of town. Phillip moved out there after his parents died right around his eighteenth birthday. They left him mostly debt. The shack had an old-fashioned burner and stove that kept him warm enough through winters. A line in the back held drying clothes washed in the river, even during freezes. His food came from his garden and trading work for supplies. Everyone else—a few with their new-fangled TVs (or at least new to our town) and the rest of us with radios and indoor electricity—couldn't imagine such a simple life. Not even a telephone.

"Who'm I gonna call?" he would respond when a few years back my neighbor Erma asked Phillip why. He said, "I can just walk down the street if I need something."

By "down the street," he meant three miles to get to the main stores and general mass of people. Our town was small, small enough to fit in one church, those who came anyway. But I couldn't imagine having no car with it all so sprawled.

After church, Phillip stayed and mingled, lunch after or not. He remembered to ask people about new babies, sick family members, and broken farm machinery. Those Blue Ridge Mountains surrounding our town, although at some distance, brought in breezy days and shadows that mixed and crossed all of our faces, except Phillip's. Somehow he just stood on out, bright. Hard to explain, but even those young like him didn't shine like that. And when he listened to answers and conversations, he leaned in, like you were the only one in the room or on that grassy hill next to the stained-glass windows. It was close to that same awe you saw during the preachings.

Phillip laughed with a hiccup and snort, like a donkey trying to cough up its morning breakfast. And he laughed often. Made other people laugh, too, with his talks about trying to rescue a cat up in some tree branches or the time he thought Maggie Smitch was on fire and he picked up her hose and let aim. Turned out she liked to dance in her saffron-and-orange scarf in the middle of the afternoon.

Now and again, a few young schoolboys would throw pebbles at him and make faces behind his back. He didn't seem to notice. Us women shook our heads at the children and gave them the eye. They hushed up until the next Sunday.

On one particular Sunday, end of spring, we all turned to go after service when someone, two someones, made their way down the road toward the church. The two figures passed by the post office, the town hall, and the bake shop. Slowly they grew from points on the road to a woman and a child—figures moving among shadowy mountains behind and above them. They left a trail of dust clouded up. None of us moved much. This was something new, something to stick around for.

The woman tugged her child along and pulled them to a stop right by the church. I don't think she meant to stop there. But everything else was closed. Population four hundred, mostly Christians, and everything stopped Saturday evenings. If she was looking for something, here was the place. She nodded at us. Her face showed tired and weary in lines from the sun and sweat touching her forehead.

Erma went up to her and put out her hand. "How do ya do?"

"Fine, thank you." The woman shook Erma's hand, but without much gumption.

"Can we help you?" asked Erma.

"I'm looking for Mr. Toby. I stopped at his shop."

"Ah, yes. Well, we're all here," said Erma. She held out her arm and swept it across the crowd and church steeple.

"Mrs. Robb? I've been expecting you." Martin leaned forward and shook the woman's hand. "I'm Martin Toby."

The woman lowered her face and shuffled her feet. Light brown hair escaped a tight, dark bonnet. The child, a girl, remained silent. Actually she looked a little dark to be this woman's child, but it was a bronzy dark, same with the hair, a deep, long chocolate. Maybe she had tanned from walking here. Nobody said anything.

"Well then, let me show you your room." Mr. Toby led the two back the way they came.

So they were Mr. Toby's new tenants. He owned the butcher shop over the hill. Since marrying Kearny Morris last year, the couple lived with Kearny's mother to take care of her. Mrs. Morris could take down any grown man to withering bits with two words. Poor man. But it meant he never used the upstairs of the building anymore.

People broke up and headed on home after that. Some stayed, though, and talked about the two, wondering where they came from and why they came here. Erma promised she would take over her usual welcome batch of raisin muffins tomorrow. From the light in Erma's eyes, those muffins would garner the real scoop.

A breeze waved my hair around and pulled out little tendrils. I tried to pat them back in place, but it was no use. Gray and white streaked through, well, more like ran over. And if anyone has hair turning, they know it isn't so nice as the hair of our youth.

Phillip sat eating an oatmeal cookie from the after-sermon snack. His eyes fixed on the road. He was off in one of his dazes. I wondered what he thought about during them.

"Do you want anything to drink?" I asked. "There's lots of iced tea left that needs drinking."

"No thank you," he said. "Seems like nice people." His eyes never left the road.

"What?"

"Mr. Toby's tenants."

172

"Oh, yes. I suppose. Don't know nothing about them."

"Well, doesn't take much to see good folks."

"I guess," I replied. *Hmm.*

He went home shortly after that. As I picked up the dirty glasses and pie plates, I watched him meander down the hill. He twirled a long stick in his hand and whistled a tune I didn't recognize. I don't think Phillip Dorsey ever thought badly about anyone. In fact, mean words got left out of his vocabulary. Not that I had anything mean to say about the woman and girl. But I thought it was odd for a woman to be moving here—no husband, no brother— so I had to assume.

Later that week, my husband got a bit of a cold, and I didn't go out for a few days. It was odd not to hear from Erma. Bob kept me busy enough, though, carrying his meals up and down stairs and getting water and new sheets and clothes. No moment passed anyway where I cared about town goings-on. Then I took sick, and on his way home from work, I made Bob get soup in a can—the only thing he knew how to fix.

Finally the next Sunday, my husband and I stepped out into a full-blown sunny day. Summer had started to creep its way into the air. Pretty soon we'd be wishing for spring again as the heat would seep into our bones and skin and hold us down in our seats. For today, it was good to see a blue sky without a cloud. As much light as those mountains poked out along the horizon line, they reflected it back from the sun and all that clear blue.

At church, ladies waved their fans back and forth in a slow dance of paper. Our preacher started late. And Erma walked in just in time for the first hymn. Even she knew better than to talk during that. The new tenants at Mr. Toby's entered around the third hymn. I sat by the aisle and saw them looking for a space. We were nearly always full up. Phillip spotted them and waved them to the space up front with him.

"What is *she* doing here?" Erma asked as soon as we stopped singing.

"What do you mean?" I whispered behind my fan.

"That girl is her daughter."

"So?"

"Never mind, I'll tell you later."

The girl hung her head in Phillip's pew. Her straw-straight, dark hair fell over her face. Her mother tapped her knee so the girl would stop fidgeting. The mother sat upright, her back like an ironing board against the pine. But her nose didn't rise with any airs. She listened intently to the preacher. Where Phillip's eyes lighted on people, hers darkened and steadied. Trailing color streams from the stained glass lifted over all three. The girl's hand closed on her mother's and broke a small smile from the woman. The girl didn't notice the look. I'm thinking she knew, though.

After services, I stayed inside collecting hymnals and Bibles. Besides, it was cooler in there without all the other bodies and those trees hanging over the church. I heard commotion outside. Loud voices slid through a propped-open window. In our crowd, that wasn't unusual. With the whole lot of churchgoers, decibels could get high. You would think there was a party every Sunday. These days, though, no one else was giving them, so I guess this was their outlet.

I picked up my pocketbook and slung it into the crook of my elbow and pinned my hat back into my bun. The wide brim covered just enough of my face to keep off the sun and heat. I didn't like to look disheveled. "Always a lady," my mama would say. Bob told me that often, either way, my face sat pretty. And each time he said it, heat moved into my cheeks.

"Well, you missed everything," said Erma. She had waddled over to me as soon as she caught me on the front church stairs.

Behind her the backs of the new woman and girl disappeared over the hill.

"Those boys. I'm afraid they upset Mrs. Robb and her daughter." Erma tsk-tsked. She whipped the day's program across her face in an attempt to stop the sweat dripping.

"Why? Whatever did they have to pick on her for?"

"I imagine her daughter instigated it. They threw mud at that girl. A leaky hose created quite the mess over by the stand of willows. Must have beckoned to the boys to play in it. I'm sure she's used to being in the mud, being that their people live in it."

"That's no call—"

"Shouldn't have brought that girl here. That's what."

"What do you mean her 'people live in it'?"

"You know, those tents they live in, right on the ground. And then they go round chanting half-naked and making ungodly body movements round fires."

My eyes widened. But Susan Frank came over to us, and Erma switched easily into another bit on one of the school teachers. Susan and I passed knowing eyes. Sometimes we had to rescue each other.

"She means the girl's Indian," Susan whispered. "She's so centered on that topic. All week long since she visited them."

I raised my eyebrow. *Well, who now cares? She still comes to church.* I just snuck on away.

"Let's go home, Bob."

He nodded and took my arm. I could feel us sticking

together. Driving away, I noticed Phillip's absence from the minglers.

I shopped every Wednesday morning and mailed letters and bills. I liked fresh fruits, and they started to come into the store now with seasons changing. The walk there made my stockings itch with the hot. A bit of steam pulled itself off the pavement. The mountain ridges popped up out of the haze and floated there: peaks, haze, slopes, haze, razored trees, haze. Summer was here. I mopped my forehead with a handkerchief my gramma gave me. It was days like these where my hats did no good. A fan in the store became an instant relief after all that.

When that little girl ran by the store window, Sunday's events moved back into my memory. I peered out the window, craning my neck. She had disappeared already. Several others ran down the street and stopped in at the town hall, where the fire department and police station kept themselves. Sirens screeched louder and closer. One of the mud-throwing boys, Landy, careened through the store's door.

"A lady's been hit. A lady's been hit." The boy rushed out again.

All of us in the store dropped our groceries and ran down the street toward the large crowd forming.

I raised up onto my tiptoes but couldn't make out who it was or if they were hurt. A path opened for the doctor. Moisture trickled down his forehead. I felt it drip down my back as well. The high sun seared my head. I had to cover my eyes from it and wipe my face and chest with my already-soaked hankie. It became a constant gesture. At a clear point, I saw Mr. Toby's tenant, the woman, lying on the road and a car with out-of-state license plates off to the side. I dropped my hand and stared.

The doctor stood up and shook his head. His arms hung by his sides and didn't move. *My God.* The woman's arms and legs sprawled out at all angles. The intersection had had many accidents, but none fatal like this. Our mayor had tried to get in a sign. But we lacked the funds.

The girl pushed back through the crowd and out, bumping people into each other. She ran with long legs that carried her away in swift kicks. Her direction seemed out of town.

The voice of a woman repeated, "I didn't see her. I didn't see her."

It wasn't until later that I thought again about the little girl. I hoped she had someplace to go. She seemed maybe ten, eleven. Bob and I had never had children of our own. So ages got clear past me.

Erma knocked on our door the next morning. Over tea, she chattered on about this woman and that man until I caught up on most everything our town had going on.

"Oh, yeah." Erma paused for a breath. "Did you see that accident yesterday? Wasn't that a pity?"

"Yes. I was in Thomson's when it happened. I can't believe she died. And just moving here and all, too. Do you know what happened to the little one?"

"Seems she vanished. She just ran. It's strange."

"They're looking for her, aren't they?"

"The sheriff sent some people out. But where would they look except the room they rented? Nothing there." She leaned on in closer to me. "He said they had nothing but the small bags they carried on their shoulders. Can you believe that? He figures her a runaway. He left the case open, though." Erma's pause was brief and on she went again. This time she covered Pastor Dean's sermon and how she had begun to take even more to heart his preachings on Jesus.

I nodded the rest of the time. My silence bothered her none.

Later after lunch, I sat out on the porch gazing at the street and neighbors, and moved my knees in and out to make the bench swing sway. The lemonade I sipped tasted too sour and didn't take the fever out of the day. Trees lined on up and down this street, nice change from the open layout of other neighborhoods. Bob picked it when we first married. Quiet and cooler than most spots. Ice cubes clinked against the glass when I set it down, my hands sliding over the wet sides. With my fan, I tried to make a draft, anything.

Down the street walked Phillip. His gray hat and slow amble told me who it was. He waved at me, slowed by my gate, but kept going. Soon the trees and the corner swallowed even his shadow. He wandered all over town usually. In fact, he stayed tan the whole year round with how often he was out, rather than his natural pale skin. But I didn't think I'd seen him down here unless he worked doing an odd chore or two for some of the older folks on our block. Soon back he came, slowing again in front of our house.

When he did that a third time, I yelled to him, "Phillip, would you like a glass of lemonade?"

Relief passed over his face and his shoulders relaxed. He took off his hat and sat on the stairs at my feet.

"Good day," he said. He took the glass I handed him and drank, more like guzzled, down the liquid. "It's a fine day."

"Yes. Hot." A headache had moved into my forehead. And

my neck felt heavy. Every limb I had to move slowed to a snail's pace.

I felt strange in the moments that followed. He didn't say a thing. Finally it was too much for me.

"I can't read your mind, Phillip," I said.

"Oh, yes. I'm sorry to be taking your time."

"Do you need something?"

"Well, there was that accident yesterday. The girl . . ."

"What about her?"

He leaned forward. "She came to me. I just don't know what to do with her."

"Came to you? You mean she's staying with you?" *At least she didn't go off the face of the earth. But still, this man with a young girl? What could he know?*

"I found her hiding in my stand of trees. She looked cold, shivering and dirty, so I got her to come inside last night. She clung to my neck so long, I thought she might not let go. She wouldn't speak much. But when I was downstairs, I heard her up in my loft, crying and mumbling."

"Sounds like you did fine. It was good of you to see to her safety, Phillip. We'll have to find her someplace else, though."

"Thank you, ma'am. I know. But she's told me she's got no family. There's no one, just her mama. Name's Elisha."

"Let me see what I can do this afternoon. I'll come out to your place after." *Now why did I go and do that?*

"Thank you. Thank you so much." Phillip tipped his hat on and off and on again.

He skirted down the road. I sighed. She's only a child, and every child needed a roof.

"There isn't any place for a child like that here."

I just stared at Erma when she said that. I knew it, too. Maybe a young couple wanted a child so badly that it didn't matter. Bob and I were too old to be raising kids now. Besides, I'd never been real comfortable around the young ones.

"We should at least ask around," I said.

"No use, I say," said Erma.

I decided I was on my own. I walked down Main Street, thinking deep. Who needed a child?

I got back a lot of shaking heads. Even Mr. Toby, with no children yet, said they were trying for their own. Many folks related the no to age or too big a family already. Erma spoke right. I hated her being right. No one wanted a child like that. In some ways, maybe I was too old to understand. Minds just weren't changing.

On the way home, I stopped in at Newberry's, the TV, radio, and basically anything else for the house store. Bob managed it during the day. Most of what people bought were the little things. It was rare to have the sale of a TV, so Bob said. Mayor had one, of course. Most folks stood outside the shopwindow to watch when anything decent happened on the screen. They crowded together, snow or heat, noses pointed at the TV, eyes focused. I told Bob we didn't need that boxy thing. And after seeing those people move into a kind of trance, faces unchanged, I knew we would never have one in our house.

"I want to drive out to Phillip's," I said to Bob. "I'll see how the girl's doing. Maybe she could stay there awhile longer."

"Seems the only thing, now." He handed me the keys to our car.

The drive out didn't take much time. I had wanted to figure a way to tell Phillip and the girl things might not work. Nobody came to mind. What was there to do?

I could corner a car like any man. Bob always got a kick out of me pulling around curves and turns with no fear. What I didn't like were the bumps on this dirt path down to Phillip's house. I held the steering wheel tight and straight, but the car and I still swayed. You'd a thought the bouncing under me would've jostled up some answer.

Nothing came to me in those ten minutes.

"Come on in," Phillip said, opening his door.

His home looked small. But the inside was clean and surprisingly neat. The stove stood in the middle with a pipe leading out to the roof. Underneath a window straight ahead sat a sink. Next to it, a shelf lined the wall with dishes, an ax, gloves, and cans of soup. On the floor by that sink lay something like a bed with old, yellowed quilts and pillows. The loft ladder leaned against a wall.

I didn't see the girl. But shadows moved up in the loft. Phillip pulled out a chair for me, and we sat at a tiny square table.

"Did you make this?" I said, fingering the rough details.

"Yes ma'am."

"This is really good," I said. "Well, I went about the town today. I'm afraid this may take longer than we thought."

"She's welcome here. Can't rush a good home."

"No, I guess not. Phillip, I talked with quite a few people. It may come about that we won't find her a home here."

"Maybe so. Maybe another town, then." The smile on his face didn't waver.

My eyes weren't passing along the message I was trying to give. I lowered my voice because I knew our voices carried upwards to small ears.

"I mean, she may need to go to a home for girls like her. Maybe an orphanage," I said.

"I doubt that. She's a good girl. She's been helping around here, cooking, gathering wood. And she's good mannered—"

"I'm sure she is. But we have to look and see that it simply might not happen."

"Well, ma'am, I tend on the positive. I know there'll be something." Again, the smile.

I sighed and pushed back from the table. "Okay. I'll keep trying for the next few days."

"Thank you. Everything will be fine." Phillip took my hand and squeezed it. The warmth spread up my wrist, and I could feel it make an appearance in my cheeks. Maybe there were a few other people I could ask.

I turned my head around the large living room. My last stop today included the mayor's wife, Millicent. They lived in the biggest house in town. Syrus George Burke had the record as the longest-sitting mayor—fifteen years.

Millicent Burke carried coffee and cups. She sat down on the edge of the high-backed chair and crossed her ankles.

We both sipped coffee for a few minutes. Seemed out of place with the air cooking. I only drank enough to be polite. The quiet reminded me of my time with Phillip. Only this time it was me who wanted something. Some of the silence came from lack of children. Their only one died at age two, a little girl. A bad flu.

"Millicent, how is Syrus doing?" I longed to say Millie. But this one didn't like nicknames.

"Fine. And Bob?"

"Good."

I sipped more coffee. The couch I sat on felt uncomfortable and looked an odd, large flower pattern. I never did agree with patterns. Didn't need them mixing with everything else. Their windows faced out to a large lawn, woods, and a tree with flowers that had just fallen.

Millicent cleared her throat. I guessed that was my cue.

"Well," I said. "Do you remember the mother and daughter who came to town a bit ago? They stayed in Martin Toby's upstairs apartment."

"Oh, yes." Her eyes got shiny.

I didn't think I'd ever seen her cry.

"What a sad thing that happened with the mother."

"That's why I'm here. You see, that little girl has no home," I said.

"No home? How is that possible?"

"She's out staying with Phillip. She told him her mom was it. No other family."

"That's terrible." Millicent pulled her skirt to straighten it so it fell to her knees. "You're not here to simply inform me, are you?"

"No. I've been all over. Everyone seems full. She can't stay with Phillip forever."

"Surely someone has room," she said.

"That's why—"

Mayor Burke walked in at that moment. His forehead crinkled. He got like that at church when he noticed kids monkeying around. That would be right before he yelled or scooted them away from each other. I had wondered what the creaking sound had been a minute ago. He'd been listening.

"Good afternoon." He nodded at me.

I nodded back. "Good afternoon. Sun's pretty hot today."

"Hmm," he said. He put a hand on his wife's shoulder. "Do you need anything, Millicent?" The hand tilted her just a bit toward him.

"No, I'm fine."

He nodded at me again—a regular habit of this man—and sauntered out of the room.

Millicent looked down at her cup and traced her finger around the rim. After a sip, she smiled. "I wish you luck."

I sighed. I guessed asking her for help was not possible. And I guessed I had been feeling it all week. My legs were starting to slip off each other, so I uncrossed them. I added some sugar to my coffee, and we moved our talk to the annual end-of-summer church social. Children created plays; adults ran booths of food, pamphlets, games, and desserts. Most of the town attended. This year's theme revolved around family and loving thy neighbor.

It took me a long time to make the drive out to Phillip's. I slowed to a snail crawl and barely hit the gas. The rocks and ruts ran on through my whole body with each moment I moved closer to the hut. How could I give him the news? And his face. The trees that lined the way, tall, thin, and with dark bark, seemed to sway in the direction I came from. Maybe they wanted me to turn back.

"She should be in an orphanage." I didn't hold it back or wait through tea. Soon as he opened the door it flew out.

"Elisha's the one come to me," he said. "She trusts me. I can't just give her off to strangers." Phillip twirled his hat in his fingers. His head hung low. I wondered what he had to be ashamed about.

"I'm sorry. But how can you take care of a little girl? What makes her better off here than in an orphanage?"

184

"I've been doing all that now two weeks. And she talks to me about her life. I listen. Will she get that in some far-off place?"

"You've been doing a fine job. But orphanages have resources and knowledge—"

"You're not understanding. She affected me." He tapped his chest with a flat hand. "I'm keeping her here if that's the only option besides sending her off."

"But she's not your kin, not your blood."

"Doesn't matter."

Past Phillip, I could see out the window. Elisha sat on a swing made from old rope and wood. She kicked her legs in and out. She swung higher than I've ever dared fly on those things. Her smile spread wide across her face, and her cheeks flushed red.

Phillip turned toward her. "She hasn't spent a day without being on that swing, even when it rains."

In town I hadn't ever seen her smile like that. Frankly, maybe I couldn't blame her. When had anyone talked to her? And had anyone given her their sympathies about her mother?

Phillip waited on Elisha while she sat under the tree next to the stained-glass window. The colors from the detailed panes moved over her dress and marked her hair. Mingling churchgoers ignored them. Conversations with Phillip had died down. Everyone had an opinion, and none of them included Elisha staying in our town. The girl swung her feet against the rock she sat on.

In my ear, all I could hear was Erma going on about the horse from Irving's farm that bucked her off. The other women circled around us and shook their heads.

"Why, Erma, you must have been a sight," said Susan. She hid a giggle behind her hand.

Coralyn tried to hide a laugh as well. "Oh yes, and in that mud from the rain."

"I can just picture skirts and boots up in the air—" Maggie interrupted her own comment with a laugh that couldn't contain itself.

We got struck with it too and let out howls and knee slaps. It was a funny sight to imagine her on the ground. I didn't see Erma join in. Her eyes seemed to fade a bit. So I stopped and patted her arm. Elisha's feet still swung, hitting the rock with *thump-thump*s.

At services no one had sat in the pew with Phillip except Elisha. But he never lost that look of awe. And he didn't seem to mind the lack of company. Elisha still sat with her head bowed and her hair over her face.

I understood that those in our town had their set ways. But what was so wrong with a little talk? It wasn't like they had to take the girl in and have her living with them. Although it'd be right in my eyes.

Stepping away from the crowd Erma had drawn, I walked over to Phillip and Elisha.

"Good afternoon," said Phillip.

"Hello," I said.

"Elisha, this is Mrs. Gilbert."

Elisha took my hand, looking at me carefully. She said hello and went back to eating a cookie. Her bites were small, and she chewed in ways to keep the crumbs in her mouth as long as possible.

"How are things?" I asked.

"Good. Good," Phillip said. "We've started to change my place around a bit, make it more comfortable. And Elisha always does the dishes and cleans up."

The man and this small child looked at each other. His eyes lit on her with pride, like how my father used to look at me. The girl held her eyes down, almost as if to push the compliment away, and yet accept it at the same time. Perhaps she never knew that kind of caring from a near stranger.

"Why don't you and your husband come by for supper Tuesday night?" Phillip said. "You've done so much for Elisha."

I hesitated. *Dinner at Phillip's?*

"We'll make apple pie for dessert. Elisha makes 'em from her mama's recipe."

Elisha peered up at me. Her eyes darkened blacker than normal the longer I took to answer. She knew what I was thinking, I was sure. Could see right through me.

"I'll talk to Bob. I'm sure we would love to."

"Seven thirty, then."

As I made my way over to Bob, I could feel Elisha's eyes on me.

I told Bob about our invitation.

"It was kind of him to include us," he said, rubbing my back. "He doesn't have much in the way of food to entertain with."

Our car thumped over a few rocks in the road. Bob drove us out this time. I wore one of my Sunday dresses and my favorite shawl. It was the scarf my mama gave me after I married. I covered my shoulders and held tight in it whenever I worried or got nervous. I thought I was both tonight as we drove to Phillip's. I didn't know why.

Was he the right person to take care of her? He was a young man, a slow one at that. But no one else wanted her. Really, no one wanted to deal with some embarrassment over her in their house. What embarrassment I wanted to know.

In my lap was my famous cold pasta salad, something to expand the dinner. A gentle wind weaved in through my rolled-down window. Finally, a cooling. The air smelled like nature cleaned herself up, like clothes after hanging on the line. I didn't want to leave the car. Bob came to the door and opened it wide. He held his hand out.

"Come on. It won't be so bad."

Elisha ran out the door.

"Phil, they're here," she yelled. She ran back inside. I could hear her excited yelps. I had never seen her with that much energy. I expect she didn't think we'd show.

Bob smiled and steered me inside. Mismatched tin and chipped china plates and cups spread across the table. Handkerchiefs were rolled like napkins. Silverware sat by each plate, the forks, knives, and spoons all in proper eating order.

It was a simple meal. The chicken probably came from ones running around his backyard. Turnips and cucumbers and corn tasted fresh from Phillip's garden. And the milk ran warm on my tongue, right from the cow's belly. I hadn't seen a cow, and I didn't ask.

"That was the best pasta salad I ever had," said Phillip. He sat back, hands over his stomach, and rocked up and back.

"Here, let me help you clean up," I said. I tried to hide my smile. Pride wasn't something I planned on displaying.

"No, ma'am. You're the guest."

But I kept right on picking up plates and so on. I waved him off with my hand. I started some water in the sink. Elisha brought me the last of the dishes and started scraping the leftovers into jars.

The wind stirred a bit more. It moved through the windows and blew loose hair out of my face. Suds dripped down my arms. Elisha dried the dishes with a threadbare cloth. The sky turned to purple and pink. I didn't know where the sun went so fast.

"That apple pie looks real good," I said. The crisscross pattern lay straight, and the strips were even. Cinnamon wafted in the air. "So, your mama taught you?"

The girl nodded.

"You're good at helping." I paused. She still didn't speak.

"Thank you." Elisha's hand touched mine when I handed her a plate. The backdrop of cloud colors turned Elisha's clothes a purple hue. It emphasized dirt stains and the too small blouse. She smiled at me, but pulled away quickly. Her copper skin glowed.

Bob and Phillip talked about repairs and gardening. Phillip wanted to add on a room, and the two men gestured and pointed with ideas.

"Elisha needs her own space," said Phillip.

"Do you like living here with Phillip?" I asked. I lowered my voice so she might feel it was more private.

She tilted her face up. Her black eyes held curiosity. "Yes, I guess I do."

"You miss your mom?"

Elisha nodded.

"Is he good to you?"

"Yes, ma'am."

Better than the rest of this town.

"He gives me more food than him," she said. "And he sleeps on the floor. He teaches me things. He let me chop wood and pull vegetables. Nobody ever showed me things like that, 'ccpt my mom."

"Do you want to stay here?" I asked.

"No one else'll take me, I presume." The black in her eyes sharpened, and her voice toughened yet wavered. "It doesn't matter. My dad used to tell me, 'Life comes for reasons. What we get is everything we need.'"

"Dad?"

"He died a while back."

"I'm sorry, Elisha. For both he and your mama."

She bowed her head. "Daddy called me Turtle." Somehow her voice echoed a strong whisper, quiet, but without any shyness. "We lived up in New York near Buffalo. Cattaraugus. We had a house like this, too. All rented, though." She shrugged. "Phillip put up the swing after I told him about my dad's."

"Fitting." She was slow to trust and move. But it was the town that acted slow accepting her . . . if they ever would. "How did he . . . go?"

"Somebody beat him. Standing up for a woman at a bar."

"Oh my." I put my arm around her. That must have been the most I'd heard her talk.

"We'll start her in school this fall, too," said Phillip.

The pit of my stomach turned. *What school? Would they let her in?*

Bob's eyes matched mine. He nodded at me.

"Let's cut into the pie," said Elisha.

Phillip pulled down plates. With them midair in his hands, he stopped.

"What is it?" asked Bob.

"Not sure."

I listened. Birds had stopped singing. Gusts whipped branches against the house. *Tap tap. Scrape.* Crickets no longer rubbed their wings together. The leaves rustled green to green.

Phillip poked his head out the window and stared into the fields.

"Get in the cellar," he whispered.

I almost didn't hear him. Elisha froze. We all seemed to recognize the tone in his voice.

"Why?" asked Elisha.

"Storm's coming." He flipped back a rug and pulled up a door. Stairs led down into the dark.

"There's candles," said Phillip. "I think it's a funnel cloud."

That moved my feet, even with his calm, slow movements. I put my arms around Elisha, and we climbed down. The air felt hollow. It tugged me backwards. Bob's shirt billowed out around him like a blue ghost. The men's words swallowed up into the atmosphere. How quickly the air changed.

I tapped around for candles and matches. My fingers trembled. But the wind would only blow out the flames.

When Phillip latched the door above us, dark took over. Yet pounding sounds only got worse. I lit the candles. I couldn't speak. It had been a long time since a storm like this rolled over our town. One happened right after Bob and I married and had come back from the honeymoon. We clung together in my mother's basement. Many houses fell to the ground under the gale forces. Mama's didn't. But it wasn't quite as recognizable afterwards.

A few minutes passed without any words. But then something perked my ears.

"Do you hear that?" I asked. My words came out like I was talking into a bottomless tin can strung to a neighbor's house.

"Yeah," said Phillip.

He rushed up the stairs and threw back the door. Candles

whipped into black. But some light filtered down. I could make out Elisha's shaking body.

Bob gathered the rest of us together closely and away from the door. The winds pushed me straight against the wall. We all squeezed hands.

Finally Phillip and a few others clunked down the steps in slow, forced moves, them against the stream. The room flipped to ink, and again I lit candles. There sat Martin and Kearny and their nephew, Sid.

"Hello," I said. I heard my voice waver.

"We saw the light on," said Martin. Dirt covered all over the three of them. "I was driving us home from taking Sid to that fair over in Fayette County. We didn't think we would be able to drive on through once we saw it."

"Thank God for small miracles," Kearny said. She touched her husband's hand for a moment and then lifted it.

Sid waved at Elisha, and she smiled. Elisha waved back. The boy readied to move closer to her, but Kearny nudged him and shook her head.

I pursed my lips and put my arm under Bob's to take his hand. Our eyes met and that was all I needed. I caught Phillip with his arm around Elisha. He kissed her on the forehead and wiped a tear on his sleeve. The girl leaned on his shoulder and closed her eyes.

What did it matter her papa could be a different makeup? *What did it matter?*

Martin and Kearny sat side by side, shoulders close to touching, but not.

When we came up the stairs, the air stood still. Particles hung in the shafts of fading light through new roof holes. I could feel grit in the back of my throat and nostrils. The door hung at an angle off its hinges. Branches littered the floor, and broken glass and plates mingled with them. The table and chairs and blankets had been flung against one wall.

Our car had shingles, boards, and branches all over it. The windshield was shattered. Bob cleaned the glass off the seat and got it to start, though. The Tobys' car, crushed by a tree, couldn't be salvaged. An oak and two pine trees had fallen across Phillip's garden as well.

"Everybody's okay," said Phillip. "That's important."

"Yeah," Elisha replied.

He nodded, and they started to pick up tree limbs.

I peered at the shabby house as we drove away. We gave the Tobys a ride. The three looked like sardines in the back, sitting tall, hands in their laps, dullness crossing their faces.

Phillip and Elisha left my porch, leftovers on plates in their hands. The two laughed and giggled down the sidewalk. They were still talking about a train trip back to her home to maybe see if she had cousins. That Phillip would always be so hopeful.

"Goodbye," I said.

Across the street, Erma waved her hand up. I signaled her over.

"They had us over last week," I said. Erma asked her normal twenty questions. She couldn't believe I'd invited *them* to dinner. The tornado veered a month in the past. Our town seemed to be getting back to its normal.

"Well, I don't know why he keeps her. It's all so tragic."

"What is?"

"The two of them together."

"She belongs with him."

193

"Well, I don't think it's right."

I hoped that the protests would remain as quiet as they had been, hands-off. No one wanted to get involved. They just wanted their town pristine the easy way. Didn't look like it would be easy for a while. But I just didn't see it. Wasn't a child always a blessing?

"You know," I said, "we could all be more like Phillip."

Erma *hmmf*ed and shuffled toward her house.

Phillip and Elisha became blurs on the horizon, disintegrating dots. They melted together, and I couldn't tell one from the other, which was short, which was tall. The three-mile walk must have taken on pleasant tones in the waning light and cooling air.

"Come sit with me," called Bob from the porch. He patted the space beside him on the swing.

We watched the stars come out, the lightning bugs flying around, our trees reaching up to hit the sky—ladders to the stars and mountaintops. We swayed back and forth, the swing creaking beneath us, in the breeze that came on, that was starting to push through.

Morning Smile

Her mother had named her from the top girls' names list twenty years previously. It meant *olive*. A food. Of all things. There was nothing behind those letters but popularity. These thoughts entered her mind as her employer spoke.

"Olivia? Do you hear me? No butter. He can't have those calories." She snapped her fingers.

The voice that penetrated her thoughts was the mother's. She really did care for her son. Really. Well, maybe. Olivia wasn't always sure.

"I got it. No cooking with butter. It's just—"

"No excuses, Olivia. We must stick to his diet." Diana stood there, a fitted black dress covering just enough to be professional. Her hair freshly curled in large, hair-sprayed waves.

Olivia would have told her there was no other way to keep the scrambled eggs from sticking. And could she get cooking spray. But the conversations usually rambled quickly and off Diana went. She and her husband, David, were house flippers and real-estate agents.

George, after little Prince George—no lie—was still asleep.

Neither Diana or David ever woke George. Nannies had been coming and going since he was born. Each one appeared to last perhaps four months, with at least four always on payroll. This was her second month.

Six fifteen. She wandered the house, so quiet sometimes she got creeped out. More so nights. The dark wood doors, window frames, and molding was typical East Ave, dating back a few hundred years. Some designer had lovingly saved the older details. Olivia ran her fingers along windowsills where the housekeeper had so carefully cleaned each nook. No dust. No spider webs.

She had until seven, George's wake-up time. Why she needed to come so early beforehand, she couldn't imagine. Hours were strict and lunches controlled. Although anything in the fridge was fair game, including the pricey Fiji water. She wondered where the liquid truly came from. The flavor was crisp, almost metallic, and clearly no Rochester pipe water.

Light shone through the back window looking out onto a small backyard and large tiled pool. Workers had only finished the house, but outside was a different story. A few boxes of tile choices sat by the pool deck.

The green back there. So green. But the bushes were thick, older, probably some English style, all about privacy. But nothing about looks.

Not what I would pick, she often thought.

She walked up the stairs, careful not to touch a foot to squeaky sections. George would be cranky all day if she woke him early. The house had so many pockets and hidden spaces, the mansion style of the area. The mother had turned a closet outside George's bedroom into the tiniest kitchen. They currently had no kitchen—the last of the reno projects. So this was it.

Stainless-steel refrigerator, sink, and dishwasher. All somehow full-size with two upper cabinets and one lower. There was a small counter, just enough for a dish strainer. Dishes couldn't be left out, though. So Olivia checked this.

Shit. That night nanny. Olivia grumbled as she put away George's dishes and even the night nanny's it seemed. Each item had a spot in either drawers or above the sink. At five foot, she had a hard time reaching the upper space. If anyone heard her grunting during this job, or cussing (not in front of George, of course), they would raise their eyebrows. But this was how she paid for her senior year at St. John Fisher College. A phone-number tab on the library wall and here she was. She started college later than most, so she felt old compared to the other nannies.

A previous nanny, Maureen, had warned her that the family was putting in nanny cams throughout George's room and the sitting room. She had pointed to the bedroom light when she told Olivia. But the house's security room showed no signs of bedroom cameras. She snuck a peek one day when the housekeeper left to answer the door.

The water drained, swirling, a motion she told George jokingly was a mini-tornado. The two often made things up. At three, he had an imagination she couldn't have possibly dreamed when she was that age.

Seven on the dot. She opened his bedroom door inch by inch. She didn't want to jolt him awake.

"George. Honey? Wake up." She whispered the words, letting them float over him. She touched his shoulder and pulled the blankets back a small bit. "George. It's time to get up."

Walking all around the room, she rolled up the shades to four large windows, so high you could see far across and down the street. Trees grew so their branches appeared as if they were about to enter the room. The shades made no sound, but light now streamed around the room.

"No," he croaked. "No light." He put his hand over his face.

"George." She sat by him, the firm mattress holding her body and his.

He opened his eyes. "Olivia!" He leaped up and wrapped arms around her. His smile was so wide, his missing front tooth showed. Another nanny had gotten in trouble for that early loss when he fell outside.

"His pictures!" Diana had exclaimed. "They'll be ruined."

She nodded when Diana said this. But Olivia held back her true thoughts. *Who cares?*

"Olivia, can we play with my trains?"

"All day if you want, buddy. We just need to eat breakfast now."

"Oh." His face fell a moment. He shrugged and then smiled again. "It's morning."

"It is!" Olivia rubbed his back. "I'm so excited to see you. Good morning, George."

"Good morning, Nanny Olivia." He lightly pulled her hair, jumped out of bed, and padded into his mini walk-in closet. "I want to wear orange today." There was room for two to stand and pick out clothes.

"Sure. You have those shorts or the tee shirt with orange in the design." She pulled both out and knew his answer.

"Both!"

They struggled getting his clothes on, mainly because he wanted to wander naked. He may have had his mother's eye for fashion, but not her desire to actually wear clothing. A few times he got loose and ran, everything jiggling and free.

"George, come on. We've got to get our day started."

"No!" He ran and ran, circling her.

"You won't get breakfast if you don't get dressed. Remember what Mama said."

"No breakfast."

Olivia sighed. She grabbed him, swinging him around, and he laughed. When she placed him on the toilet, he stopped.

"No, Olivia. I can't go now."

"Just try. It's been all night."

"I think I went in my Pull-Ups."

She blew hair out of her face and kneeled until the slow tinkle streamed down into the toilet.

"Excellent, buddy. Good job." They high-fived.

Once finally dressed, Olivia brought him an egg, avocado, orange slices, and milk. He ate the avocado and egg, drinking milk down in between. She had to take the milk away so he didn't fill up on that alone.

They walked the neighborhood, him almost too big now for the stroller, his legs hanging, nearly touching the sidewalk. But Olivia knew George wouldn't get far on foot. Just going down the street to the small playground outside a school, he asked at least twice that he be carried. His dad was six four. The little boy was growing faster than his age could keep up.

They browsed pastry and chocolate shops, trendy boutiques, and restaurants. Mostly window-shopping. She didn't want him eating sweets, neither did his mom, and she didn't have extra money. College. Books. Coffee shops. All had her wallet.

"Let's go back, buddy." They neared the block's end, and her legs had tired. His weight was heavy pushed that long.

His nonresponse made her peek under the black shade. Out. Nap time. His mother wasn't going to like a morning nap.

The house loomed large and gloomy in a back corner, with an English air about it. Dark, heavy wood, gray brick, and the largest front doors she had ever seen. They reminded her of those doors she had seen in gothic movies with extraordinarily large door knockers and strange carvings. Here, there were only carvings along the sides and corners. She didn't think they wanted people knocking with something that might wear down the wood.

He woke as soon as they entered and "front door open" followed by a loud beep sounded while the door creaked opened.

"Home, Olivia?"

"Home, George. You hungry?"

"Ummm, yes."

The afternoon flew by quickly with postlunch coloring, puzzles, and a woozy food coma leading to another nap.

Diana came home early. Popping in unannounced wasn't unusual. "Hello, Olivia. Everything go okay?" She didn't look at Olivia, but flipped through notes she had taken that day regarding George. Daily journals were required.

"Good. He'll be asleep for another half hour."

"Okay. Just in time for dinner. We're taking him out with friends. Be sure he's dressed appropriately."

"Of course."

"You'd be more than welcome to come. Kate canceled tonight." Diana showed her dimpled smile, but it was tight. The tone was strained with deeper notes. She was exhausted.

"I'm afraid I have a summer class." Dodged. George eating out was a nightmare.

"Oh, I see. You are always welcome to take on more hours. We might need that."

"Okay." Olivia gulped. Sweat trickled down her sides. Even

the meanest teacher hadn't ever made her this nervous. But this woman had her stomach flipping.

"Oh, yes." Diana's voice and demeanor changed. Almost . . . cheered up. Brightened. "I got this the other day. You're Iroquois, right?"

"Seneca, yes." *What is this?*

"This postcard came. Apparently your tribe is putting on a festival." Her fingernails were rounded and pointed at the same time in the lightest pink shade. When she put her hands on her hips, they flashed with the light. "You'll be there of course, I suspect."

"It's been going on for over twenty years. This year, I'll be watching George." Olivia was surprised his mother even brought it up. She didn't usually tell bosses or coworkers her background. She wanted to avoid the whole "oh that's so cool you're Native." But Diana had been talking about George's family tree and his blood ties to King Charles II and had asked her about it naturally in conversation.

"Oh. That's too bad. Maybe we can work something out. Switch hours with someone else."

"It's okay. I knew it wouldn't work with my assigned days." She couldn't tell if Diana was being genuine or hoping that Olivia would work anyway. This woman was good at this.

"Nonsense. It's done. You will switch hours. I'll have the housekeeper figure it out with you."

"Oh." Olivia felt confused. She had worried this might cause trouble being so new. Her left hand shook. Even after she told the mother she was Seneca that one night of ancestors and family trees, Diana hadn't asked much. She simply nodded and went back to drawing the lines. Olivia never thought this would matter to her.

"I've got to get to a meeting. I just wanted to check in. I'll be back in time for the dinner." Diana half smiled. Then she was gone. So often just a fading image.

Olivia lightly slapped her face and then gulped down a Fiji water. Cooling.

She heard George stir through the baby monitor. He cooed when he stretched, or sometimes when he dreamed. The sound could be that, too.

His door made creaking sounds even when slowly opened. "Shhh," she said to the door. He wasn't awake but close, as his eyes fluttered.

"George?"

His baby blues appeared, and his smile turned up his whole face. "Olivia!"

"Hi, sweetie." She laughed and tickled him.

"Stop, stop." But he laughed even more.

"Off to a nice dinner tonight. What do you want to wear?"

"Hmm." He put his finger on his chin. Something his mother did. Olivia saw her in George's head tilt and his facial expressions. His dad also mirrored in George's gangly, tall three-year-old build. "Blue pants and white buttons-up?" His dimple appeared when he said "buttons."

"Add a tie and you've got an outfit."

Another struggle. When the doors later shut behind her and Olivia drove her car out of the driveway, his calls after her echoed. The housekeeper pulled him back. It wasn't unusual for his parents to arrive later than the time agreed. The housekeeper would have to stay as Olivia couldn't be late.

She had put George down an hour ago. The house grew dark. A very black dark. The security alarm had been turned on so she had to stay upstairs in his suite or out in the long hallway. But she couldn't move elsewhere without great noise, phone calls, and possibly police.

The railings had been smoothed and stained deep chocolate, a perfection only money could buy. There were no bumps as she ran her hands along the wood. The renovation of the staircase alone must have been in the high thousands. Olivia never saw that much money spent at once. Those intricate carvings moved flowers and vines down the staircase.

Her mother and father had made her and her brother a clean, safe home in the town of Greece, the west side. They never wanted for anything. But she didn't get the real Cabbage Patch doll when she was seven. A Muppets lunch box had been on sale, so she got that. The only time she experienced pop music was the radio, her grandmother's older one with a record player, and the records her kindergarten teacher played at nap time.

That teacher, Miss Ananaya, was probably why she loved caring for children. She made that age so fun. A court-jester's wand. Play-Doh. Chocolate milk. *Charlotte's Web*, with voices of course.

A loud banging began. Somewhere near the parents' bedroom. She hated going in there, such a private space. There it was again.

Olivia's heart beat faster. She grabbed a mop from the hall closet and tiptoed over. She flung the door open and flipped lights on.

Nothing.

There the banging went again. In their closet. More the mother's closet. Again, the door flew open with her fast hands.

Olivia pointed her phone, the flashlight app lighting corners. Until one corner she caught orange.

"Hey there," she said. She picked up a large tabby cat with

brilliant orange fur. George would love this animal. "What are you doing in there?"

Olivia walked back to George's sitting room. Somehow, though, her movements set off the alarm. Or *something* did.

Shit. What is the passcode? She racked her brain as she ran for the phone. The cat she dropped on the couch. *Passcode. Passcode.*

"Hello?"

"Yes. We're calling about an alarm at 20 Crescent Lane. Do you have the passcode?"

"Umm. I think . . . oh, is it *Michigan*?" Diana's home state.

"No. Ma'am, we need the right passcode."

"I'm so sorry. I'm the nanny. I don't know how the alarm went off. I stayed upstairs." Olivia's eyes welled with tears. Her entire body shook.

"Ma'am, we have to send someone there. They're on their way."

"Okay."

The doorbell rang. *Already?*

She ran down the grand staircase, her shoes pounding hard.

"Ma'am? We're responding to an alarm." The two men were in police uniforms. They had pads of paper ready with pens.

"I know. I couldn't remember the passcode. I'm Olivia, the nanny." She held out her hand. They didn't reach back.

"We need to see your ID," one officer said.

Up the stairs, then back, she showed them.

"You're not the owner on file."

"Well, no." She looked behind her. Would this wake up George? Would they call Diana and David? "Wait," she said. "Hang on. Is the passcode *this great nation*?" David said that all the time. Weird. Something about being a Roosevelt fan.

The two men looked at each other.

"Yes," said the only officer who spoke.

"Phew. We good now? You didn't call them, did you?"

"We called them after you couldn't give the passcode."

"Oh my God. They'll be so mad."

"Have a good evening, ma'am." The officer tipped his hat, his face somber.

When they left, the alarm finally stopped. She reset it and ran upstairs. But it went off again. *For the love of Pete*. This time, she gave them the right passcode.

Five minutes later, his parents were home.

"Are you okay, Olivia?" Diana said. She put her hands on Olivia's shoulders.

"Yes. I don't know what set it off. I'm so sorry I didn't remember the code."

"Did they check the house?"

"No."

"David, go check around. Were you up here the whole time?"

"Yes, only up here." She motioned with her hand.

David checked everywhere. Olivia pointed out the cat to Diana.

"Good grief. How did that thing get in here?" She sniffed and raised her nose.

Olivia knew the cat would be in a pound that night. "I'll see you next week."

"Wait, what?" said David. "You're coming in tomorrow, right?"

"No, it's the Ganondagan Festival. Diana had me change my hours so I could volunteer."

"Oh. That's right. I did," Diana said.

"But we don't have a nanny tomorrow," said David. His hands formed fists that opened and closed.

"What happened to Lisa, the new girl?" Olivia asked. Her heart pounded.

"She canceled. That's twice this week. And on a Saturday." She sighed. "So we let her go." Diana straightened the blanket on the couch, refolding the material at an angle.

David turned to Olivia. "We need you tomorrow. So you'll come in." He walked away, headed to his bedroom.

"I'm sorry, Olivia. He's right."

Before she could refuse, the two were gone. Olivia clenched her hands. She wanted to punch the perfectly fluffed pillows. But she held back. She blasted her music on the drive home, instead.

Olivia rang the doorbell at six a.m. Saturday morning didn't mean a later time. She rang again. Then waited in her car. This happened a lot, even though she wasn't allowed a key. At seven, Diana answered the doorbell intercom, sounding like sleep still held her. "I'll be right there."

She opened the door. "Good morning, Olivia. Remember, no butter."

Olivia rolled her eyes. She usually tried to hold those back. But too tired to care, she trudged upstairs, set her stuff down, and woke George.

"Olivia!" He smiled, his dimples making small pockets. George hugged her. "You're again here."

"Yup. I wanted to see you two days in a row!"

"Good. Now let's get my outfit."

Olivia laughed. Anger rolled away as the day passed. She didn't forget the festival or the duties she'd backed out on. But

George kept her busy. And she played for him some social dance music.

"That's really great, Olivia. Can we dance?"

"No, not here. But if you go to the festival, you can." She tickled him, and his giggles carried. He almost lost breath. But he asked for more.

"Olivia." Diana's tone was stern. Olivia didn't know how long she had stood there. "Let's talk."

The two stood in the tiny kitchen, no room to turn.

"I don't think you should tickle him. He gets too excited."

"Okay. Sure, Diana." Olivia's heart sank. Sometimes George asked for tickles or tickled her. He was just a kid.

"Let's also tone down the music." So she'd been there awhile.

"Of course." Olivia let her voice get stern.

"Okay. That's all. I'm grateful you could stay today." She touched Olivia's arm and then left.

She sighed in relief when their car left. "Story time, George."

"Yeah!"

When the couple returned that night, Olivia was reading. George had been tucked away hours ago. David went straight to their bedroom, which was strange. He loved TV. But he appeared tired.

"Long night?" asked Diana.

"Not too bad." She packed her books up and grabbed her purse.

"We'll see you tomorrow." Diana sighed.

"Umm, no, I won't be here."

Diana raised her eyebrows. She looked about to cry.

"I have my volunteering tomorrow. I can't miss again as it puts a strain on the festival."

Halfway out the door, Olivia turned back. "You might consider bringing George. He likes our music. And by the way, his morning smile is the greatest thing. You should see it sometime."

No other words were exchanged.

I'm so fired. Done.

Olivia waved at Marley. The woman drove by in the golf carts Olivia envied every year. They looked like fun. But she wandered the stations, filling in where needed. Always the floater.

"Can you go organize the dancers?" Bernadette asked. "Make sure they're good to go."

"Sure."

"Why aren't you dancing this year?" she asked.

Olivia shrugged. "I thought I had to work."

"They should know you'll be here."

"Next year."

Bernadette nodded and started talking into her walkie-talkie.

The dancers seemed okay. They all asked where her regalia was and why she wasn't dancing. Olivia finally left. Walking up the hill, she heard her name.

Weird. Maybe Bernadette needed something.

"Olivia!" George ran and literally bumped into her, hugging her legs.

"George? What are you doing here?"

"Mama told me we could come." He motioned his thumb toward his mom. Diana waved.

"Oh, hi."

"Olivia. Good to see you."

"Mama. We got to go see that longhouse. That lady was talking about it."

"Okay. Well, give me a moment with Olivia."

George ran circles around them.

"This is great. I didn't know this was here."

She watched the mother stare off into the distance. She looked nervous. "It's not near Park Ave," Olivia said.

"Far from it."

The pause was long. The sound hung there between them. People talked. Drums beat. Cooking meat sizzled. A child cried. Peter, the site manager of Ganondagan, picked up the microphone in the main tent. He invited people to watch the dancers.

"Dancing is starting."

"Dancing?" said George. "Oh, Mama. Olivia. Let's go." He pulled them both.

"Olivia has to work right now, George."

George beamed his smile.

"I think I can make some time." Olivia poked his nose. A small bubble of excitement built. Maybe hope.

George giggled.

The two each held one of his hands. They both walked slower than George. Behind him, in similar strides. Diana gave Olivia a smile that had potential, maybe even a realness about it. The big tent stood over them, feet stomping the stage, singers singing, rattles rattling.

Dancing Girl

They watch her small feet. Shuffle shuffle shuffle. When she bends over, her small dress reveals a diaper. The girl plucks grass and giggles. Then she catches up with her mother.

Adult women smile. How cute is this little girl running around.

Her mother holds out her hand. Come on, sweetie. Follow us. She shows her daughter steps. The girl copies the best she can. Tap tap. Shuffle.

She twirls when the drummers speed up the songs. Arms outstretched, face to the sky, sun heating her cheeks pink.

Her feet have become steady. The patterns more clear. Shuffle, tilt, shuffle, move hips, dip with the notes. The girl wears a traditional top, purple calico with black ribbons. Ponytail drawing back hair. Other girls move and she watches. She copies them. Her mother chats with other women, bobbing her head with the music. Nodding approval toward her.

She calls out the song where words repeat and refrain. Like a habit, she knows them but doesn't understand meaning. She tilts more, following music, following drummers, following dancers.

Off to the side, the girls sit at picnic tables, giggling, whispering.

Her mother calls her. Girls, join us. She waves them over.

The girls roll their eyes and shake their heads.

She sees her mother dance. How she tilts, looks at the sun, the trees, the other dancers. Her mother's moves are slower than before, but deliberate, a cadence. The breeze pushes back her hair. She notices her mother laugh with another woman. They lean in, smile, then follow the men and other women. Stomping. Stomping. Shaking the ground. Faces turning serious.

She feels that vibration, hears the sound, notices the birds land near them, and the trees bend and sway. But the girl holds tight to the table.

Her hair is so much longer. She twists the ends and throws them behind her. Moccasins hold her feet, make them steady, tied to the ground. Jeans stretch. The song tells the Creation Story, and they recreate shuffle, shuffle, pat, pat. Drums flow through her blood; the blood pumps to the beat. She grasps her belly and thinks of Sky Woman. Her body tilts and sways and her arms wing out. She turns and follows. The men's singing calls out, throbbing, rattles shaking.

Moves shape her. Make her. Learned habits she would remember, her body sometimes when she can't. Ingrained. Her feet to the earth. Her feet to the earth.

Acknowledgments

I am grateful to all of those who guided me through crucial times and who showed me how words can make a difference. I learned from others how to unsilence those moments often left hanging in the air.

Thank you to the Amerind Museum for the time to reflect and write; to Alyea Canada, my editor, who believed so strongly in these stories and so kindly thought about the lines; to the Feminist Press for first seeing something in this book and for loving it to fruition; to Ganondagan for always teaching; to Gathering of Good Minds for keeping us in our better minds and relationships and always thinking as family; to Writers & Books for that early space to know other writers, to explore words freely, to teach others, and to read "Phillip"; to what has become and remains my home city, no matter how far away I am, Rochester—you are a space that slows down and embraces the arts; to Maria Brandt, Julie Johnson, and Toni Jensen for comments on early drafts; to various writing groups across the years; to those at readings who desired my book in print and wanted to buy the book right then; and to all of the tossed-out stories, images, and lines.

The errors and infelicities of language are mine. I impart them in loyalty to the characters, the closeness to their voices, and the orality of bringing realities to these stories. There is a cadence and a rhythm to how we all speak every day, to how we speak in certain groups and communities, and to how we relate with one another. My attempt here was to think about that orality in story, although imperfect in execution. It's a process breaking the rules and expectations set into our minds through education systems about Western language and sentence rules. But here we are, moving forward, sliding through the syllables, around the commas, and into the voice. Our voices. Translated into the sound and the images.

More Contemporary Fiction from the Feminist Press

La Bastarda by Trifonia Melibea Obono, translated by Lawrence Schimel

Black Wave by Michelle Tea

Fade Into You by Nikki Darling

Give It to Me by Ana Castillo

Go Home! edited by Rowan Hisayo Buchanan

Into the Go-Slow by Bridgett M. Davis

Love War Stories by Ivelisse Rodriguez

Maggie Terry by Sarah Schulman

Pretty Things by Virginie Despentes, translated by Emma Ramadan

Since I Laid My Burden Down by Brontez Purnell

Though I Get Home by YZ Chin

Training School for Negro Girls by Camille Acker

We Were Witches by Ariel Gore

The Feminist Press is a nonprofit educational organization founded to amplify feminist voices. FP publishes classic and new writing from around the world, creates cutting-edge programs, and elevates silenced and marginalized voices in order to support personal transformation and social justice for all people.

See our complete list of books at
feministpress.org